Madame Delphine

&

Bylow Hill

George W. Cable

Madame Delphine & Bylow Hill

The present edition is a reproduction of previous publication of this classic work. Minor typographical errors may have been corrected without note, however, for an authentic reading experience the spelling, punctuation, and capitalization have been retained from the original text.

ISBN: 978-1-64799-394-8

CONTENTS

MADAME DELPHINE

BYLOW HILL

MADAME DELPHINE

CHAPTER I

AN OLD HOUSE

A few steps from the St. Charles Hotel, in New Orleans, brings you to and across Canal street, the central avenue of the city, and to that corner where the flower-women sit at the inner and outer edges of the arcaded sidewalk, and make the air sweet with their fragrant merchandise. The crowd—and if it is near the time of the carnival it will be great—will follow Canal street.

But you turn, instead, into the quiet, narrow way which a lover of Creole antiquity, in fondness for a romantic past, is still prone to call the Rue Royale. You will pass a few restaurants, a few auction rooms, a few furniture warehouses, and will hardly realize that you have left behind you the activity and clatter of a city of merchants before you find yourself in a region of architectural decrepitude, where an ancient and foreign-seeming domestic life, in second stories, overhangs the ruins of a former commercial prosperity, and upon everything has settled down a long Sabbath of decay. The vehicles in the street are few in number, and are merely passing through; the stores are shrunken into shops; you see here and there, like a patch of bright mould, the stall of that significant fungus, the Chinaman. Many great doors are shut and clamped and grown gray with cobweb; many street windows are nailed up; half the balconies are begrimed and rust-eaten, and many of the humid arches and alleys which characterize the older Franco-Spanish piles of stuccoed brick betray a squalor almost oriental.

Yet beauty lingers here. To say nothing of the picturesque, sometimes you get sight of comfort, sometimes of opulence, through the unlatched wicket in some porte-cochère—red-painted brick

1

pavement, foliage of dark palm or pale banana, marble or granite masonry and blooming parterres; or through a chink between some pair of heavy batten window-shutters, opened with an almost reptile wariness, your eye gets a glimpse of lace and brocade upholstery, silver and bronze, and much similar rich antiquity.

The faces of the inmates are in keeping; of the passengers in the street a sad proportion are dingy and shabby; but just when these are putting you off your guard, there will pass you a woman—more likely two or three—of patrician beauty.

Now, if you will go far enough down this old street, you will see, as you approach its intersection with——. Names in that region elude one like ghosts.

However, as you begin to find the way a trifle more open, you will not fail to notice on the right-hand side, about midway of the square, a small, low, brick house of a story and a half, set out upon the sidewalk, as weather-beaten and mute as an aged beggar fallen asleep. Its corrugated roof of dull red tiles, sloping down toward you with an inward curve, is overgrown with weeds, and in the fall of the year is gay with the yellow plumes of the golden-rod. You can almost touch with your cane the low edge of the broad, overhanging eaves. The batten shutters at door and window, with hinges like those of a postern, are shut with a grip that makes one's knuckles and nails feel lacerated. Save in the brick-work itself there is not a cranny. You would say the house has the lock-jaw. There are two doors, and to each a single chipped and battered marble step. Continuing on down the sidewalk, on a line with the house, is a garden masked from view by a high, close board-fence. You may see the tops of its fruit-trees—pomegranate, peach, banana, fig, pear, and particularly one large orange, close by the fence, that must be very old.

The residents over the narrow way, who live in a three-story house, originally of much pretension, but from whose front door hard times have removed almost all vestiges of paint, will tell you:

"Yass, de 'ouse is in'abit; 'tis live in."

And this is likely to be all the information you get—not that they would not tell, but they cannot grasp the idea that you wish to know—until, possibly, just as you are turning to depart, your informant, in a single word and with the most evident non-appreciation of its value, drops the simple key to the whole matter:

"Dey's quadroons."

He may then be aroused to mention the better appearance of the place in former years, when the houses of this region generally stood farther apart, and that garden comprised the whole square.

2

Here dwelt, sixty years ago and more, one Delphine Carraze; or, as she was commonly designated by the few who knew her, Madame Delphine. That she owned her home, and that it had been given her by the then deceased companion of her days of beauty, were facts so generally admitted as to be, even as far back as that sixty years ago, no longer a subject of gossip. She was never pointed out by the denizens of the quarter as a character, nor her house as a "feature." It would have passed all Creole powers of guessing to divine what you could find worthy of inquiry concerning a retired quadroon woman; and not the least puzzled of all would have been the timid and restive Madame Delphine herself.

CHAPTER II

MADAME DELPHINE

During the first quarter of the present century, the free quadroon caste of New Orleans was in its golden age. Earlier generations—sprung, upon the one hand, from the merry gallants of a French colonial military service which had grown gross by affiliation with Spanish-American frontier life, and, upon the other hand, from comely Ethiopians culled out of the less negroidal types of African live goods, and bought at the ship's side with vestiges of quills and cowries and copper wire still in their head-dresses,—these earlier generations, with scars of battle or private rencontre still on the fathers, and of servitude on the manumitted mothers, afforded a mere hint of the splendor that was to result from a survival of the fairest through seventy-five years devoted to the elimination of the black pigment and the cultivation of hyperian excellence and nymphean grace and beauty. Nor, if we turn to the present, is the evidence much stronger which is offered by the gens de couleur whom you may see in the quadroon quarter this afternoon, with "Ichabod" legible on their murky foreheads through a vain smearing of toilet powder, dragging their chairs down to the narrow gate-way of their close-fenced gardens, and staring shrinkingly at you as you pass, like a nest of yellow kittens.

But as the present century was in its second and third decades, the quadroones (for we must contrive a feminine spelling to define the strict limits of the caste as then established) came forth in splendor. Old travellers spare no terms to tell their praises, their faultlessness of feature, their perfection of form, their varied styles of beauty,—for there were even pure Caucasian blondes among them,—their fascinating manners, their sparkling vivacity, their chaste and pretty wit, their grace in the dance, their modest propriety, their taste and elegance in dress. In the gentlest and most poetic sense they were indeed the sirens of this land, where it seemed "always afternoon"—a momentary triumph of an Arcadian over a Christian civilization, so beautiful and so seductive that it

4

became the subject of special chapters by writers of the day more original than correct as social philosophers.

The balls that were got up for them by the male sang-pur were to that day what the carnival is to the present. Society balls given the same nights proved failures through the coincidence. The magnates of government,—municipal, state, federal,—those of the army, of the learned professions and of the clubs,—in short, the white male aristocracy in everything save the ecclesiastical desk,— were there. Tickets were high-priced to insure the exclusion of the vulgar. No distinguished stranger was allowed to miss them. They were beautiful! They were clad in silken extenuations from the throat to the feet, and wore, withal, a pathos in their charm that gave them a family likeness to innocence.

Madame Delphine, were you not a stranger, could have told you all about it; though hardly, I suppose, without tears.

But at the time of which we would speak (1821-22) her day of splendor was set, and her husband—let us call him so for her sake— was long dead. He was an American, and, if we take her word for it, a man of noble heart and extremely handsome; but this is knowledge which we can do without.

Even in those days the house was always shut, and Madame Delphine's chief occupation and end in life seemed to be to keep well locked up in-doors. She was an excellent person, the neighbors said,—a very worthy person; and they were, may be, nearer correct than they knew. They rarely saw her save when she went to or returned from church; a small, rather tired-looking, dark quadroone of very good features and a gentle thoughtfulness of expression which it would take long to describe: call it a widow's look.

In speaking of Madame Delphine's house, mention should have been made of a gate in the fence on the Royal-street sidewalk. It is gone now, and was out of use then, being fastened once for all by an iron staple clasping the cross-bar and driven into the post.

Which leads us to speak of another person.

CHAPTER III

CAPITAINE LEMAITRE

He was one of those men that might be any age,—thirty, forty, forty-five; there was no telling from his face what was years and what was only weather. His countenance was of a grave and quiet, but also luminous, sort, which was instantly admired and ever afterward remembered, as was also the fineness of his hair and the blueness of his eyes. Those pronounced him youngest who scrutinized his face the closest. But waiving the discussion of age, he was odd, though not with the oddness that he who reared him had striven to produce.

He had not been brought up by mother or father. He had lost both in infancy, and had fallen to the care of a rugged old military grandpa of the colonial school, whose unceasing endeavor had been to make "his boy" as savage and ferocious a holder of unimpeachable social rank as it became a pure-blooded French Creole to be who could trace his pedigree back to the god Mars.

"Remember, my boy," was the adjuration received by him as regularly as his waking cup of black coffee, "that none of your family line ever kept the laws of any government or creed." And if it was well that he should bear this in mind, it was well to reiterate it persistently, for, from the nurse's arms, the boy wore a look, not of docility so much as of gentle, judicial benevolence. The domestics of the old man's house used to shed tears of laughter to see that look on the face of a babe. His rude guardian addressed himself to the modification of this facial expression; it had not enough of majesty in it, for instance, or of large dare-deviltry; but with care these could be made to come.

And, true enough, at twenty-one (in Ursin Lemaitre), the labors of his grandfather were an apparent success. He was not rugged, nor was he loud-spoken, as his venerable trainer would have liked to present him to society; but he was as serenely terrible as a well-aimed rifle, and the old man looked upon his results with pride. He had cultivated him up to that pitch where he scorned to practice any vice, or any virtue, that did not include the principle of

6

self-assertion. A few touches only were wanting here and there to achieve perfection, when suddenly the old man died. Yet it was his proud satisfaction, before he finally lay down, to see Ursin a favored companion and the peer, both in courtesy and pride, of those polished gentlemen famous in history, the brothers Lafitte.

The two Lafittes were, at the time young Lemaitre reached his majority (say 1808 or 1812), only merchant blacksmiths, so to speak, a term intended to convey the idea of blacksmiths who never soiled their hands, who were men of capital, stood a little higher than the clergy, and moved in society among its autocrats. But they were full of possibilities, men of action, and men, too, of thought, with already a pronounced disbelief in the custom-house. In these days of big carnivals they would have been patented as the dukes of Little Manchac and Barataria.

Young Ursin Lemaitre (in full the name was Lemaitre-Vignevielle) had not only the hearty friendship of these good people, but also a natural turn for accounts; and as his two friends were looking about them with an enterprising eye, it easily resulted that he presently connected himself with the blacksmithing profession. Not exactly at the forge in the Lafittes' famous smithy, among the African Samsons, who, with their shining black bodies bared to the waist, made the Rue St. Pierre ring with the stroke of their hammers; but as a—there was no occasion to mince the word in those days—smuggler.

Smuggler—patriot—where was the difference? Beyond the ken of a community to which the enforcement of the revenue laws had long been merely so much out of every man's pocket and dish, into the all-devouring treasury of Spain. At this date they had come under a kinder yoke, and to a treasury that at least echoed when the customs were dropped into it; but the change was still new. What could a man be more than Capitaine Lemaitre was—the soul of honor, the pink of courtesy, with the courage of the lion, and the magnanimity of the elephant; frank—the very exchequer of truth! Nay, go higher still: his paper was good in Toulouse street. To the gossips in the gaming-clubs he was the culminating proof that smuggling was one of the sublimer virtues.

Years went by. Events transpired which have their place in history. Under a government which the community by and by saw was conducted in their interest, smuggling began to lose its respectability and to grow disreputable, hazardous, and debased. In certain onslaughts made upon them by officers of the law, some of the smugglers became murderers. The business became unprofitable for a time until the enterprising Lafittes—thinkers—bethought them of a corrective—"privateering."

7

Thereupon the United States Government set a price upon their heads. Later yet it became known that these outlawed pirates had been offered money and rank by Great Britain if they would join her standard, then hovering about the water-approaches to their native city, and that they had spurned the bribe; wherefore their heads were ruled out of the market, and, meeting and treating with Andrew Jackson, they were received as lovers of their country, and as compatriots fought in the battle of New Orleans at the head of their fearless men, and—here tradition takes up the tale—were never seen afterward.

Capitaine Lemaitre was not among the killed or wounded, but he was among the missing.

CHAPTER IV

THREE FRIENDS

The roundest and happiest-looking priest in the city of New Orleans was a little man fondly known among his people as Père Jerome. He was a Creole and a member of one of the city's leading families. His dwelling was a little frame cottage, standing on high pillars just inside a tall, close fence, and reached by a narrow outdoor stair from the green batten gate. It was well surrounded by crape myrtles, and communicated behind by a descending stair and a plank-walk with the rear entrance of the chapel over whose worshippers he daily spread his hands in benediction. The name of the street—ah! there is where light is wanting. Save the Cathedral and the Ursulines, there is very little of record concerning churches at that time, though they were springing up here and there. All there is certainty of is that Père Jerome's frame chapel was some little new-born "down-town" thing, that may have survived the passage of years, or may have escaped "Paxton's Directory" "so as by fire." His parlor was dingy and carpetless; one could smell distinctly there the vow of poverty. His bedchamber was bare and clean, and the bed in it narrow and hard; but between the two was a dining-room that would tempt a laugh to the lips of any who looked in. The table was small, but stout, and all the furniture of the room substantial, made of fine wood, and carved just enough to give the notion of wrinkling pleasantry. His mother's and sister's doing, Père Jerome would explain; they would not permit this apartment—or department—to suffer. Therein, as well as in the parlor, there was odor, but of a more epicurean sort, that explained interestingly the Père Jerome's rotundity and rosy smile.

In this room, and about this miniature round table, used sometimes to sit with Père Jerome two friends to whom he was deeply attached—one, Evariste Varrillat, a playmate from early childhood, now his brother-in-law; the other, Jean Thompson, a companion from youngest manhood, and both, like the little priest himself, the regretful rememberers of a fourth comrade who was a

9

comrade no more. Like Père Jerome, they had come, through years, to the thick of life's conflicts,—the priest's brother-in-law a physician, the other an attorney, and brother-in-law to the lonely wanderer,—yet they loved to huddle around this small board, and be boys again in heart while men in mind. Neither one nor another was leader. In earlier days they had always yielded to him who no longer met with them a certain chieftainship, and they still thought of him and talked of him, and, in their conjectures, groped after him, as one of whom they continued to expect greater things than of themselves.

They sat one day drawn thus close together, sipping and theorizing, speculating upon the nature of things in an easy, bold, sophomoric way, the conversation for the most part being in French, the native tongue of the doctor and priest, and spoken with facility by Jean Thompson the lawyer, who was half Américain; but running sometimes into English and sometimes into mild laughter. Mention had been made of the absentee.

Père Jerome advanced an idea something like this:

"It is impossible for any finite mind to fix the degree of criminality of any human act or of any human life. The Infinite One alone can know how much of our sin is chargeable to us, and how much to our brothers or our fathers. We all participate in one another's sins. There is a community of responsibility attaching to every misdeed. No human since Adam—nay, nor Adam himself— ever sinned entirely to himself. And so I never am called upon to contemplate a crime or a criminal but I feel my conscience pointing at me as one of the accessories."

"In a word," said Evariste Varrillat, the physician, "you think we are partly to blame for the omission of many of your Paternosters, eh?"

Father Jerome smiled.

"No; a man cannot plead so in his own defense; our first father tried that, but the plea was not allowed. But, now, there is our absent friend. I tell you truly this whole community ought to be recognized as partners in his moral errors. Among another people, reared under wiser care and with better companions, how different might he not have been! How can we speak of him as a law-breaker who might have saved him from that name?" Here the speaker turned to Jean Thompson, and changed his speech to English. "A lady sez to me to-day: 'Père Jerome, 'ow dat is a dreadfool dat 'e gone at de coas' of Cuba to be one corsair! Aint it?' 'Ah, Madame,' I sez, "tis a terrible! I'ope de good God will fo'give me an' you fo' dat!'"

Jean Thompson answered quickly:

"You should not have let her say that."

"Mais, fo' w'y?"

"Why, because, if you are partly responsible, you ought so much the more to do what you can to shield his reputation. You should have said,"—the attorney changed to French,—"'He is no pirate; he has merely taken out letters of marque and reprisal under the flag of the republic of Carthagena!'"

"Ah, bah!" exclaimed Doctor Varrillat, and both he and his brother-in-law, the priest, laughed.

"Why not?" demanded Thompson.

"Oh!" said the physician, with a shrug, "say id thad way iv you wand."

Then, suddenly becoming serious, he was about to add something else, when Père Jerome spoke.

"I will tell you what I could have said. I could have said: 'Madame, yes; 'tis a terrible fo' him. He stum'le in de dark; but dat good God will mek it a mo' terrible fo' dat man, oohever he is, w'at put 'at light out!'"

"But how do you know he is a pirate?" demanded Thompson, aggressively.

"How do we know?" said the little priest, returning to French. "Ah! there is no other explanation of the ninety-and-nine stories that come to us, from every port where ships arrive from the north coast of Cuba, of a commander of pirates there who is a marvel of courtesy and gentility——"* [*See Gazettes of the period.

"And whose name is Lafitte," said the obstinate attorney.

"And who, nevertheless, is not Lafitte," insisted Père Jerome.

"Daz troo, Jean," said Doctor Varrillat. "We hall know daz troo."

Père Jerome leaned forward over the board and spoke, with an air of secrecy, in French.

"You have heard of the ship which came into port here last Monday. You have heard that she was boarded by pirates, and that the captain of the ship himself drove them off."

"An incredible story," said Thompson.

"But not so incredible as the truth. I have it from a passenger. There was on the ship a young girl who was very beautiful. She came on deck, where the corsair stood, about to issue his orders, and, more beautiful than ever in the desperation of the moment, confronted him with a small missal spread open, and, her finger on the Apostles' Creed, commanded him to read. He read it, uncovering his head as he read, then stood gazing on her face, which did not quail; and then, with a low bow, said: 'Give me this book and I will do your bidding.' She gave him the book and bade him leave the ship, and he left it unmolested."

11

Père Jerome looked from the physician to the attorney and back again, once or twice, with his dimpled smile.

"But he speaks English, they say," said Jean Thompson.

"He has, no doubt, learned it since he left us," said the priest.

"But this ship-master, too, says his men called him Lafitte."

"Lafitte? No. Do you not see? It is your brother-in-law, Jean Thompson! It is your wife's brother! Not Lafitte, but" (softly) "Lemaitre! Lemaitre! Capitaine Ursin Lemaitre!"

The two guests looked at each other with a growing drollery on either face, and presently broke into a laugh.

"Ah!" said the doctor, as the three rose up, "you juz kip dad cog-an'-bull fo' yo' negs summon."

Père Jerome's eyes lighted up—

"I goin' to do it!"

"I tell you," said Evariste, turning upon him with sudden gravity, "iv dad is troo, I tell you w'ad is sure-sure! Ursin Lemaitre din kyare nut'n fo' doze creed; he fall in love!"

Then, with a smile, turning to Jean Thompson, and back again to Père Jerome:

"But anny'ow you tell it in dad summon dad 'e kyare fo' dad creed."

Père Jerome sat up late that night, writing a letter. The remarkable effects upon a certain mind, effects which we shall presently find him attributing solely to the influences of surrounding nature, may find for some a more sufficient explanation in the fact that this letter was but one of a series, and that in the rover of doubted identity and incredible eccentricity Père Jerome had a regular correspondent.

12

CHAPTER V

THE CAP FITS

About two months after the conversation just given, and therefore somewhere about the Christmas holidays of the year 1821, Père Jerome delighted the congregation of his little chapel with the announcement that he had appointed to preach a sermon in French on the following Sabbath—not there, but in the cathedral.

He was much beloved. Notwithstanding that among the clergy there were two or three who shook their heads and raised their eyebrows, and said he would be at least as orthodox if he did not make quite so much of the Bible and quite so little of the dogmas, yet "the common people heard him gladly." When told, one day, of the unfavorable whispers, he smiled a little and answered his informant,—whom he knew to be one of the whisperers himself,—laying a hand kindly upon his shoulder:

"Father Murphy,"—or whatever the name was,—"your words comfort me."

"How is that?"

"Because—*'Væ quum benedixerint mihi homines!'*"[1]

The appointed morning, when it came, was one of those exquisite days in which there is such a universal harmony, that worship rises from the heart like a spring.

"Truly," said Père Jerome to the companion who was to assist him in the mass, "this is a Sabbath day which we do not have to make holy, but only to keep so."

May be it was one of the secrets of Père Jerome's success as a preacher, that he took more thought as to how he should feel, than as to what he should say.

The cathedral of those days was called a very plain old pile, boasting neither beauty nor riches; but to Père Jerome it was very lovely; and before its homely altar, not homely to him, in the performance of those solemn offices, symbols of heaven's mightiest truths, in the hearing of the organ's harmonies, and the yet more

---

[1] "Woe unto me, when all men speak well of me!"

13

eloquent interunion of human voices in the choir, in overlooking the worshipping throng which knelt under the soft, chromatic lights, and in breathing the sacrificial odors of the chancel, he found a deep and solemn joy; and yet I guess the finest thought of his soul the while was one that came thrice and again:

"Be not deceived, Père Jerome, because saintliness of feeling is easy here; you are the same priest who overslept this morning, and overate yesterday, and will, in some way, easily go wrong to-morrow and the day after."

He took it with him when—the Veni Creator sung—he went into the pulpit. Of the sermon he preached, tradition has preserved for us only a few brief sayings, but they are strong and sweet.

"My friends," he said,—this was near the beginning,—"the angry words of God's book are very merciful—they are meant to drive us home; but the tender words, my friends, they are sometimes terrible! Notice these, the tenderest words of the tenderest prayer that ever came from the lips of a blessed martyr—the dying words of the holy Saint Stephen, 'Lord, lay not this sin to their charge.' Is there nothing dreadful in that? Read it thus: 'Lord, lay not this sin to their charge.' Not to the charge of them who stoned him? To whose charge then? Go ask the holy Saint Paul. Three years afterward, praying in the temple at Jerusalem, he answered that question: 'I stood by and consented.' He answered for himself only; but the Day must come when all that wicked council that sent Saint Stephen away to be stoned, and all that city of Jerusalem, must hold up the hand and say: 'We, also, Lord—we stood by.' Ah! friends, under the simpler meaning of that dying saint's prayer for the pardon of his murderers is hidden the terrible truth that we all have a share in one another's sins."

Thus Père Jerome touched his key-note. All that time has spared us beside may be given in a few sentences.

"Ah!" he cried once, "if it were merely my own sins that I had to answer for, I might hold up my head before the rest of mankind; but no, no, my friends—we cannot look each other in the face, for each has helped the other to sin. Oh, where is there any room, in this world of common disgrace, for pride? Even if we had no common hope, a common despair ought to bind us together and forever silence the voice of scorn!"

And again, this:

"Even in the promise to Noë, not again to destroy the race with a flood, there is a whisper of solemn warning. The moral account of the antediluvians was closed off and the balance brought down in the year of the deluge; but the account of those who come

14

after runs on and on, and the blessed bow of promise itself warns us that God will not stop it till the Judgment Day! O God, I thank thee that that day must come at last, when thou wilt destroy the world, and stop the interest on my account!"

It was about at this point that Père Jerome noticed, more particularly than he had done before, sitting among the worshippers near him, a small, sad-faced woman, of pleasing features, but dark and faded, who gave him profound attention. With her was another in better dress, seemingly a girl still in her teens, though her face and neck were scrupulously concealed by a heavy veil, and her hands, which were small, by gloves.

"Quadroones," thought he, with a stir of deep pity.

Once, as he uttered some stirring word, he saw the mother and daughter (if such they were), while they still bent their gaze upon him, clasp each other's hand fervently in the daughter's lap. It was at these words:

"My friends, there are thousands of people in this city of New Orleans to whom society gives the ten commandments of God with all the nots rubbed out! Ah! good gentlemen! if God sends the poor weakling to purgatory for leaving the right path, where ought some of you to go who strew it with thorns and briers!"

The movement of the pair was only seen because he watched for it. He glanced that way again as he said:

"O God, be very gentle with those children who would be nearer heaven this day had they never had a father and mother, but had got their religious training from such a sky and earth as we have in Louisiana this holy morning! Ah! my friends, nature is a big-print catechism!"

The mother and daughter leaned a little farther forward, and exchanged the same spasmodic hand-pressure as before. The mother's eyes were full of tears.

"I once knew a man," continued the little priest, glancing to a side aisle where he had noticed Evariste and Jean sitting against each other, "who was carefully taught, from infancy to manhood, this single only principle of life: defiance. Not justice, not righteousness, not even gain; but defiance: defiance to God, defiance to man, defiance to nature, defiance to reason; defiance and defiance and defiance."

"He is going to tell it!" murmured Evariste to Jean.

"This man," continued Père Jerome, "became a smuggler and at last a pirate in the Gulf of Mexico. Lord, lay not that sin to his charge alone! But a strange thing followed. Being in command of men of a sort that to control required to be kept at the austerest

15

distance, he now found himself separated from the human world and thrown into the solemn companionship with the sea, with the air, with the storm, the calm, the heavens by day, the heavens by night. My friends, that was the first time in his life that he ever found himself in really good company.

"Now, this man had a great aptness for accounts. He had kept them—had rendered them. There was beauty, to him, in a correct, balanced, and closed account. An account unsatisfied was a deformity. The result is plain. That man, looking out night after night upon the grand and holy spectacle of the starry deep above and the watery deep below, was sure to find himself, sooner or later, mastered by the conviction that the great Author of this majestic creation keeps account of it; and one night there came to him, like a spirit walking on the sea, the awful, silent question: 'My account with God—how does it stand?' Ah! friends, that is a question which the book of nature does not answer.

"Did I say the book of nature is a catechism? Yes. But, after it answers the first question with 'God,' nothing but questions follow; and so, one day, this man gave a ship full of merchandise for one little book which answered those questions. God help him to understand it! and God help you, monsieur and you, madame, sitting here in your smuggled clothes, to beat upon the breast with me and cry, 'I, too, Lord—I, too, stood by and consented.'"

Père Jerome had not intended these for his closing words; but just there, straight away before his sight and almost at the farthest door, a man rose slowly from his seat and regarded him steadily with a kind, bronzed, sedate face, and the sermon, as if by a sign of command, was ended. While the Credo was being chanted he was still there; but when, a moment after its close, the eye of Père Jerome returned in that direction, his place was empty.

As the little priest, his labor done and his vestments changed, was turning into the Rue Royale and leaving the cathedral out of sight, he just had time to understand that two women were purposely allowing him to overtake them, when the one nearer him spoke in the Creole patois, saying, with some timid haste:

"Good-morning, Père—Père Jerome; Père Jerome, we thank the good God for that sermon."

"Then, so do I," said the little man. They were the same two that he had noticed when he was preaching. The younger one bowed silently; she was a beautiful figure, but the slight effort of Père Jerome's kind eyes to see through the veil was vain. He would presently have passed on, but the one who had spoken before said:

"I thought you lived in the Rue des Ursulines."

16

"Yes; I am going this way to see a sick person."

The woman looked up at him with an expression of mingled confidence and timidity.

"It must be a blessed thing to be so useful as to be needed by the good God," she said.

Père Jerome smiled:

"God does not need me to look after his sick; but he allows me to do it, just as you let your little boy in frocks carry in chips." He might have added that he loved to do it, quite as much.

It was plain the woman had somewhat to ask, and was trying to get courage to ask it.

"You have a little boy?" asked the priest.

"No, I have only my daughter;" she indicated the girl at her side. Then she began to say something else, stopped, and with much nervousness asked:

"Père Jerome, what was the name of that man?"

"His name?" said the priest. "You wish to know his name?"

"Yes, Monsieur" (or Miché, as she spoke it); "it was such a beautiful story." The speaker's companion looked another way.

"His name," said Father Jerome,—"some say one name and some another. Some think it was Jean Lafitte, the famous; you have heard of him? And do you go to my church, Madame——?"

"No, Miché; not in the past; but from this time, yes. My name"—she choked a little, and yet it evidently gave her pleasure to offer this mark of confidence—"is Madame Delphine—Delphine Carraze."

17

CHAPTER VI

A CRY OF DISTRESS

Père Jerome's smile and exclamation, as some days later he entered his parlor in response to the announcement of a visitor, were indicative of hearty greeting rather than surprise.

"Madame Delphine!"

Yet surprise could hardly have been altogether absent, for though another Sunday had not yet come around, the slim, smallish figure sitting in a corner, looking very much alone, and clad in dark attire, which seemed to have been washed a trifle too often, was Delphine Carraze on her second visit. And this, he was confident, was over and above an attendance in the confessional, where he was sure he had recognized her voice.

She rose bashfully and gave her hand, then looked to the floor, and began a faltering speech, with a swallowing motion in the throat, smiled weakly and commenced again, speaking, as before, in a gentle, low note, frequently lifting up and casting down her eyes, while shadows of anxiety and smiles of apology chased each other rapidly across her face. She was trying to ask his advice.

"Sit down," said he; and when they had taken seats she resumed, with downcast eyes:

"You know,—probably I should have said this in the confessional, but—

"No matter, Madame Delphine; I understand; you did not want an oracle, perhaps; you want a friend."

She lifted her eyes, shining with tears, and dropped them again.

"I"—she ceased. "I have done a"—she dropped her head and shook it despondingly—"a cruel thing." The tears rolled from her eyes as she turned away her face.

Père Jerome remained silent, and presently she turned again, with the evident intention of speaking at length.

"It began nineteen years ago—by"—her eyes, which she had lifted, fell lower than ever, her brow and neck were suffused with blushes, and she murmured—"I fell in love."

18

She said no more, and by and by Père Jerome replied:

"Well, Madame Delphine, to love is the right of every soul. I believe in love. If your love was pure and lawful I am sure your angel guardian smiled upon you; and if it was not, I cannot say you have nothing to answer for, and yet I think God may have said: 'She is a quadroone; all the rights of her womanhood trampled in the mire, sin made easy to her—almost compulsory,—charge it to account of whom it may concern."

"No, no!" said Madame Delphine, looking up quickly, "some of it might fall upon—" Her eyes fell, and she commenced biting her lips and nervously pinching little folds in her skirt. "He was good—as good as the law would let him be—better, indeed, for he left me property, which really the strict law does not allow. He loved our little daughter very much. He wrote to his mother and sisters, owning all his error and asking them to take the child and bring her up. I sent her to them when he died, which was soon after, and did not see my child for sixteen years. But we wrote to each other all the time, and she loved me. And then—at last—" Madame Delphine ceased speaking, but went on diligently with her agitated fingers, turning down foolish hems lengthwise of her lap.

"At last your mother-heart conquered," said Père Jerome.

She nodded.

"The sisters married, the mother died; I saw that even where she was she did not escape the reproach of her birth and blood, and when she asked me to let her come—." The speaker's brimming eyes rose an instant. "I know it was wicked, but—I said, come."

The tears dripped through her hands upon her dress.

"Was it she who was with you last Sunday?"

"Yes."

"And now you do not know what to do with her?"

"Ah! c'est ça, oui!—that is it."

"Does she look like you, Madame Delphine?"

"Oh, thank God, no! you would never believe she was my daughter; she is white and beautiful!"

"You thank God for that which is your main difficulty, Madame Delphine."

"Alas! yes."

Père Jerome laid his palms tightly across his knees with his arms bowed out, and fixed his eyes upon the ground, pondering.

"I suppose she is a sweet, good daughter?" said he, glancing at Madame Delphine without changing his attitude.

Her answer was to raise her eyes rapturously.

19

"Which gives us the dilemma in its fullest force," said the priest, speaking as if to the floor. "She has no more place than if she had dropped upon a strange planet." He suddenly looked up with a brightness which almost as quickly passed away, and then he looked down again. His happy thought was the cloister; but he instantly said to himself: "They cannot have overlooked that choice, except intentionally—which they have a right to do." He could do nothing but shake his head.

"And suppose you should suddenly die," he said; he wanted to get at once to the worst.

The woman made a quick gesture, and buried her head in her handkerchief, with the stifled cry:

"Oh, Olive, my daughter!"

"Well, Madame Delphine," said Père Jerome, more buoyantly, "one thing is sure: we must find a way out of this trouble."

"Ah!" she exclaimed, looking heavenward, "if it might be!"

"But it must be!" said the priest.

"But how shall it be?" asked the desponding woman.

"Ah!" said Père Jerome, with a shrug, "God knows."

"Yes," said the quadroone, with a quick sparkle in her gentle eye; "and I know, if God would tell anybody, He would tell you!"

The priest smiled and rose.

"Do you think so? Well, leave me to think of it. I will ask Him."

"And He will tell you!" she replied. "And He will bless you!" She rose and gave her hand. As she withdrew it she smiled. "I had such a strange dream," she said, backing toward the door.

"Yes?"

"Yes. I got my troubles all mixed up with your sermon. I dreamed I made that pirate the guardian of my daughter."

Père Jerome smiled also, and shrugged.

"To you, Madame Delphine, as you are placed, every white man in this country, on land or on water, is a pirate, and of all pirates, I think that one is, without doubt, the best."

"Without doubt," echoed Madame Delphine, wearily, still withdrawing backward. Père Jerome stepped forward and opened the door.

The shadow of some one approaching it from without fell upon the threshold, and a man entered, dressed in dark blue cottonade, lifting from his head a fine Panama hat, and from a broad, smooth brow, fair where the hat had covered it and dark below, gently stroking back his very soft, brown locks. Madame Delphine slightly started aside, while Père Jerome reached silently, but eagerly, forward, grasped a larger hand than his own, and motioned its owner to a seat. Madame Delphine's eyes ventured no higher than to discover that the shoes of the visitor were of white duck.

"Well, Père Jerome," she said, in a hurried under-tone, "I am just going to say Hail Marys all the time till you find that out for me!"

"Well, I hope that will be soon, Madame Carraze. Good-day, Madame Carraze."

And as she departed, the priest turned to the new-comer and extended both hands, saying, in the same familiar dialect in which he had been addressing the quadroone:

"Well-a-day, old playmate! After so many years!"

They sat down side by side, like husband and wife, the priest playing with the other's hand, and talked of times and seasons past, often mentioning Evariste and often Jean.

Madame Delphine stopped short half-way home and returned to Père Jerome's. His entry door was wide open and the parlor door ajar. She passed through the one and with downcast eyes was standing at the other, her hand lifted to knock, when the door was drawn open and the white duck shoes passed out. She saw, besides, this time the blue cottonade suit.

"Yes," the voice of Père Jerome was saying, as his face appeared in the door—"Ah! Madame—"

"I lef' my parasol," said Madame Delphine, in English.

There was this quiet evidence of a defiant spirit hidden somewhere down under her general timidity, that, against a fierce conventional prohibition, she wore a bonnet instead of the turban of her caste, and carried a parasol.

Père Jerome turned and brought it.

He made a motion in the direction in which the late visitor had disappeared.

"Madame Delphine, you saw dat man?"

"Not his face."

"You couldn' billieve me iv I tell you w'at dat man purpose to do!"

"Is dad so, Père Jerome?"

"He's goin' to hopen a bank!"

"Ah!" said Madame Delphine, seeing she was expected to be astonished.

Père Jerome evidently longed to tell something that was best kept secret; he repressed the impulse, but his heart had to say something. He threw forward one hand and looking pleasantly at

21

Madame Delphine, with his lips dropped apart, clenched his extended hand and thrusting it toward the ground, said in a solemn under-tone:

"He is God's own banker, Madame Delphine."

CHAPTER VII

MICHÉ VIGNEVIELLE

Madame Delphine sold one of the corner lots of her property. She had almost no revenue, and now and then a piece had to go. As a consequence of the sale, she had a few large bank-notes sewed up in her petticoat, and one day—may be a fortnight after her tearful interview with Père Jerome—she found it necessary to get one of these changed into small money. She was in the Rue Toulouse, looking from one side to the other for a bank which was not in that street at all, when she noticed a small sign hanging above a door, bearing the name "Vignevielle." She looked in. Père Jerome had told her (when she had gone to him to ask where she should apply for change) that if she could only wait a few days, there would be a new concern opened in Toulouse street,—it really seemed as if Vignevielle was the name, if she could judge; it looked to be, and it was, a private banker's,—"U. L. Vignevielle's," according to a larger inscription which met her eyes as she ventured in. Behind the counter, exchanging some last words with a busy-mannered man outside, who, in withdrawing, seemed bent on running over Madame Delphine, stood the man in blue cottonade, whom she had met in Père Jerome's door-way. Now, for the first time, she saw his face, its strong, grave, human kindness shining softly on each and every bronzed feature. The recognition was mutual. He took pains to speak first, saying, in a re-assuring tone, and in the language he had last heard her use:

"'Ow I kin serve you, Madame?"

"Iv you pliz, to mague dad bill change, Miché."

She pulled from her pocket a wad of dark cotton handkerchief, from which she began to untie the imprisoned note. Madame Delphine had an uncommonly sweet voice, and it seemed so to strike Monsieur Vignevielle. He spoke to her once or twice more, as he waited on her, each time in English, as though he enjoyed the humble melody of its tone, and presently, as she turned to go, he said:

23

"Madame Carraze!"

She started a little, but bethought herself instantly that he had heard her name in Père Jerome's parlor. The good father might even have said a few words about her after her first departure; he had such an overflowing heart.

"Madame Carraze," said Monsieur Vignevielle, "doze kine of note wad you 'an' me juz now is bein' contrefit. You muz tek kyah from doze kine of note. You see—" He drew from his cash-drawer a note resembling the one he had just changed for her, and proceeded to point out certain tests of genuineness. The counterfeit, he said, was so and so.

"Bud," she exclaimed, with much dismay, "dad was de manner of my bill! Id muz be—led me see dad bill wad I give you,—if you pliz, Miché."

Monsieur Vignevielle turned to engage in conversation with an employé and a new visitor, and gave no sign of hearing Madame Delphine's voice. She asked a second time, with like result, lingered timidly, and as he turned to give his attention to a third visitor, reiterated:

"Miché Vignevielle, I wizh you pliz led——"

"Madame Carraze," he said, turning so suddenly as to make the frightened little woman start, but extending his palm with a show of frankness, and assuming a look of benignant patience, "'ow I kin fine doze note now, mongs' all de rez? Iv you pliz nod to mague me doze troub'."

The dimmest shadow of a smile seemed only to give his words a more kindly authoritative import, and as he turned away again with a manner suggestive of finality, Madame Delphine found no choice but to depart. But she went away loving the ground beneath the feet of Monsieur U. L. Vignevielle.

"Oh, Père Jerome!" she exclaimed in the corrupt French of her caste, meeting the little father on the street a few days later, "you told the truth that day in your parlor. Mo conné li à c't heure. I know him now; he is just what you called him."

"Why do you not make him your banker, also, Madame Delphine?"

"I have done so this very day!" she replied, with more happiness in her eyes than Père Jerome had ever before seen there.

"Madame Delphine," he said, his own eyes sparkling, "make him your daughter's guardian; for myself, being a priest, it would not be best; but ask him; I believe he will not refuse you."

Madame Delphine's face grew still brighter as he spoke.

"It was in my mind," she said.

24

Yet to the timorous Madame Delphine many trifles became, one after another, an impediment to the making of this proposal, and many weeks elapsed before further delay was positively without excuse. But at length, one day in May, 1822, in a small private office behind Monsieur Vignevielle's banking-room,—he sitting beside a table, and she, more timid and demure than ever, having just taken a chair by the door,—she said, trying, with a little bashful laugh, to make the matter seem unimportant, and yet with some tremor of voice:

"Miché Vignevielle, I bin maguing my will." (Having commenced their acquaintance in English, they spoke nothing else.)

"'Tis a good idy," responded the banker.

"I kin mague you de troub' to kib dad will fo' me, Miché Vignevielle?"

"Yez."

She looked up with grateful re-assurance; but her eyes dropped again as she said:

"Miché Vignevielle——" Here she choked, and began her peculiar motion of laying folds in the skirt of her dress, with trembling fingers. She lifted her eyes, and as they met the look of deep and placid kindness that was in his face, some courage returned, and she said:

"Miché."

"Wad you wand?" asked he, gently.

"If it arrive to me to die——"

"Yez?"

Her words were scarcely audible:

"I wand you teg kyah my lill' girl."

"You 'ave one lill' gal, Madame Carraze?"

She nodded with her face down.

"An' you godd some mo' chillen?"

"No."

"I nevva know dad, Madame Carraze. She's a lill' small gal?"

Mothers forget their daughters' stature. Madame Delphine said:

"Yez."

For a few moments neither spoke, and then Monsieur Vignevielle said:

"I will do dad."

"Lag she been you' h-own?" asked the mother, suffering from her own boldness.

"She's a good lill' chile, eh?"

"Miché, she's a lill' hangel!" exclaimed Madame Delphine, with a look of distress.

"Yez; I teg kyah 'v 'er, lag my h-own. I mague you dad promise."

"But——" There was something still in the way, Madame Delphine seemed to think.

The banker waited in silence.

"I suppose you will want to see my lill' girl?"

He smiled; for she looked at him as if she would implore him to decline.

"Oh, I tek you' word fo' hall dad, Madame Carraze. It mague no differend wad she loog lag; I don' wan' see 'er."

Madame Delphine's parting smile—she went very shortly—was gratitude beyond speech.

Monsieur Vignevielle returned to the seat he had left, and resumed a newspaper,—the Louisiana Gazette in all probability,—which he had laid down upon Madame Delphine's entrance. His eyes fell upon a paragraph which had previously escaped his notice. There they rested. Either he read it over and over unwearyingly, or he was lost in thought. Jean Thompson entered.

"Now," said Mr. Thompson, in a suppressed tone, bending a little across the table, and laying one palm upon a package of papers which lay in the other, "it is completed. You could retire from your business any day inside of six hours without loss to anybody." (Both here and elsewhere, let it be understood that where good English is given the words were spoken in good French.)

Monsieur Vignevielle raised his eyes and extended the newspaper to the attorney, who received it and read the paragraph. Its substance was that a certain vessel of the navy had returned from a cruise in the Gulf of Mexico and Straits of Florida, where she had done valuable service against the pirates—having, for instance, destroyed in one fortnight in January last twelve pirate vessels afloat, two on the stocks, and three establishments ashore.

"United States brig Porpoise," repeated Jean Thompson. "Do you know her?"

"We are acquainted," said Monsieur Vignevielle.

CHAPTER VIII

SHE

A quiet footstep, a grave new presence on financial sidewalks, a neat garb slightly out of date, a gently strong and kindly pensive face, a silent bow, a new sign in the Rue Toulouse, a lone figure with a cane, walking in meditation in the evening light under the willows of Canal Marigny, a long-darkened window re-lighted in the Rue Conti—these were all; a fall of dew would scarce have been more quiet than was the return of Ursin Lemaitre-Vignevielle to the precincts of his birth and early life.

But we hardly give the event its right name. It was Capitaine Lemaitre who had disappeared; it was Monsieur Vignevielle who had come back. The pleasures, the haunts, the companions, that had once held out their charms to the impetuous youth, offered no enticements to Madame Delphine's banker. There is this to be said even for the pride his grandfather had taught him, that it had always held him above low indulgences; and though he had dallied with kings, queens, and knaves through all the mazes of Faro, Rondeau, and Craps, he had done it loftily; but now he maintained a peaceful estrangement from all. Evariste and Jean, themselves, found him only by seeking.

"It is the right way," he said to Père Jerome, the day we saw him there. "Ursin Lemaitre is dead. I have buried him. He left a will. I am his executor."

"He is crazy," said his lawyer brother-in-law, impatiently.

"On the contr-y," replied the little priest, "'e 'as come ad hisse'f."

Evariste spoke.

"Look at his face, Jean. Men with that kind of face are the last to go crazy."

"You have not proved that," replied Jean, with an attorney's obstinacy. "You should have heard him talk the other day about that newspaper paragraph. 'I have taken Ursin Lemaitre's head; I have it

27

with me; I claim the reward, but I desire to commute it to citizenship.' He is crazy."

Of course Jean Thompson did not believe what he said; but he said it, and, in his vexation, repeated it, on the banquettes and at the clubs; and presently it took the shape of a sly rumor, that the returned rover was a trifle snarled in his top-hamper.

This whisper was helped into circulation by many trivial eccentricities of manner, and by the unaccountable oddness of some of his transactions in business.

"My dear sir!" cried his astounded lawyer, one day, "you are not running a charitable institution!"

"How do you know?" said Monsieur Vignevielle. There the conversation ceased.

"Why do you not found hospitals and asylums at once," asked the attorney, at another time, with a vexed laugh, "and get the credit of it?"

"And make the end worse than the beginning," said the banker, with a gentle smile, turning away to a desk of books.

"Bah!" muttered Jean Thompson.

Monsieur Vignevielle betrayed one very bad symptom. Wherever he went he seemed looking for somebody. It may have been perceptible only to those who were sufficiently interested in him to study his movements; but those who saw it once saw it always. He never passed an open door or gate but he glanced in; and often, where it stood but slightly ajar, you might see him give it a gentle push with his hand or cane. It was very singular.

He walked much alone after dark. The guichinangoes (garroters, we might say), at those times the city's particular terror by night, never crossed his path. He was one of those men for whom danger appears to stand aside.

One beautiful summer night, when all nature seemed hushed in ecstasy, the last blush gone that told of the sun's parting, Monsieur Vignevielle, in the course of one of those contemplative, uncompanioned walks which it was his habit to take, came slowly along the more open portion of the Rue Royale, with a step which was soft without intention, occasionally touching the end of his stout cane gently to the ground and looking upward among his old acquaintances, the stars.

It was one of those southern nights under whose spell all the sterner energies of the mind cloak themselves and lie down in bivouac, and the fancy and the imagination, that cannot sleep, slip their fetters and escape, beckoned away from behind every flowering bush and sweet-smelling tree, and every stretch of lonely, half-lighted walk, by the genius of poetry. The air stirred softly now and then, and was still again, as if the breezes lifted their expectant pinions and lowered them once more, awaiting the rising of the moon in a silence which fell upon the fields, the roads, the gardens, the walls, and the suburban and half-suburban streets, like a pause in worship. And anon she rose.

Monsieur Vignevielle's steps were bent toward the more central part of the town, and he was presently passing along a high, close, board-fence, on the right-hand side of the way, when, just within this inclosure, and almost overhead, in the dark boughs of a large orange-tree, a mocking-bird began the first low flute-notes of his all-night song. It may have been only the nearness of the songster that attracted the passer's attention, but he paused and looked up.

And then he remarked something more,—that the air where he had stopped was filled with the overpowering sweetness of the night-jasmine. He looked around; it could only be inside the fence. There was a gate just there. Would he push it, as his wont was? The grass was growing about it in a thick turf, as though the entrance had not been used for years. An iron staple clasped the cross-bar, and was driven deep into the gate-post. But now an eye that had been in the blacksmithing business—an eye which had later received high training as an eye for fastenings—fell upon that staple, and saw at a glance that the wood had shrunk from it, and it had sprung from its hold, though without falling out. The strange habit asserted itself; he laid his large hand upon the cross-bar; the turf at the base yielded, and the tall gate was drawn partly open.

At that moment, as at the moment whenever he drew or pushed a door or gate, or looked in at a window, he was thinking of one, the image of whose face and form had never left his inner vision since the day it had met him in his life's path and turned him face about from the way of destruction.

The bird ceased. The cause of the interruption, standing within the opening, saw before him, much obscured by its own numerous shadows, a broad, ill-kept, many-flowered garden, among whose untrimmed rose-trees and tangled vines, and often, also, in its old walks of pounded shell, the coco-grass and crab-grass had spread riotously, and sturdy weeds stood up in bloom. He stepped in and drew the gate to after him. There, very near by, was the clump of jasmine, whose ravishing odor had tempted him. It stood just beyond a brightly moonlit path, which turned from him in a curve toward the residence, a little distance to the right, and escaped the view at a point where it seemed more than likely a door

29

of the house might open upon it. While he still looked, there fell upon his ear, from around that curve, a light footstep on the broken shells,—one only, and then all was for a moment still again. Had he mistaken? No. The same soft click was repeated nearer by, a pale glimpse of robes came through the tangle, and then, plainly to view, appeared an outline—a presence—a form—a spirit—a girl!

From throat to instep she was as white as Cynthia. Something above the medium height, slender, lithe, her abundant hair rolling in dark, rich waves back from her brows and down from her crown, and falling in two heavy plaits beyond her round, broadly girt waist and full to her knees, a few escaping locks eddying lightly on her graceful neck and her temples,—her arms, half hid in a snowy mist of sleeve, let down to guide her spotless skirts free from the dewy touch of the grass,—straight down the path she came!

Will she stop? Will she turn aside? Will she espy the dark form in the deep shade of the orange, and, with one piercing scream, wheel and vanish? She draws near. She approaches the jasmine; she raises her arms, the sleeves falling like a vapor down to the shoulders; rises upon tiptoe, and plucks a spray. O Memory! Can it be? Can it be? Is this his quest, or is it lunacy? The ground seems to M. Vignevielle the unsteady sea, and he to stand once more on a deck. And she? As she is now, if she but turn toward the orange, the whole glory of the moon will shine upon her face. His heart stands still; he is waiting for her to do that. She reaches up again; this time a bunch for her mother. That neck and throat! Now she fastens a spray in her hair. The mocking-bird cannot withhold; he breaks into song—she turns—she turns her face—it is she, it is she! Madame Delphine's daughter is the girl he met on the ship.

CHAPTER IX

OLIVE

She was just passing seventeen—that beautiful year when the heart of the maiden still beats quickly with the surprise of her new dominion, while with gentle dignity her brow accepts the holy coronation of womanhood. The forehead and temples beneath her loosely bound hair were fair without paleness, and meek without languor. She had the soft, lacklustre beauty of the South; no ruddiness of coral, no waxen white, no pink of shell; no heavenly blue in the glance; but a face that seemed, in all its other beauties, only a tender accompaniment for the large, brown, melting eyes, where the openness of child-nature mingled dreamily with the sweet mysteries of maiden thought. We say no color of shell on face or throat; but this was no deficiency, that which took its place being the warm, transparent tint of sculptured ivory.

This side door-way which led from Madame Delphine's house into her garden was overarched partly by an old remnant of vine-covered lattice, and partly by a crape-myrtle, against whose small, polished trunk leaned a rustic seat. Here Madame Delphine and Olive loved to sit when the twilights were balmy or the moon was bright.

"Chérie," said Madame Delphine on one of these evenings, "why do you dream so much?"

She spoke in the patois most natural to her, and which her daughter had easily learned.

The girl turned her face to her mother, and smiled, then dropped her glance to the hands in her own lap, which were listlessly handling the end of a ribbon. The mother looked at her with fond solicitude. Her dress was white again; this was but one night since that in which Monsieur Vignevielle had seen her at the bush of night-jasmine. He had not been discovered, but had gone away, shutting the gate, and leaving it as he had found it.

Her head was uncovered. Its plaited masses, quite black in the moonlight, hung down and coiled upon the bench, by her side. Her chaste drapery was of that revived classic order which the world of fashion was again laying aside to re-assume the mediæval bondage of the stay-lace; for New Orleans was behind the fashionable world, and Madame Delphine and her daughter were behind New Orleans. A delicate scarf, pale blue, of lightly netted worsted, fell from either shoulder down beside her hands. The look that was bent upon her changed perforce to one of gentle admiration. She seemed the goddess of the garden.

Olive glanced up. Madame Delphine was not prepared for the movement, and on that account repeated her question:

"What are you thinking about?"

The dreamer took the hand that was laid upon hers between her own palms, bowed her head, and gave them a soft kiss.

The mother submitted. Wherefore, in the silence which followed, a daughter's conscience felt the burden of having withheld an answer, and Olive presently said, as the pair sat looking up into the sky:

"I was thinking of Père Jerome's sermon."

Madame Delphine had feared so. Olive had lived on it ever since the day it was preached. The poor mother was almost ready to repent having ever afforded her the opportunity of hearing it. Meat and drink had become of secondary value to her daughter; she fed upon the sermon.

Olive felt her mother's thought and knew that her mother knew her own; but now that she had confessed, she would ask a question:

"Do you think, maman, that Père Jerome knows it was I who gave that missal?"

"No," said Madame Delphine, "I am sure he does not."

Another question came more timidly:

"Do—do you think he knows him?"

"Yes, I do. He said in his sermon he did."

Both remained for a long time very still, watching the moon gliding in and through among the small dark-and-white clouds. At last the daughter spoke again.

"I wish I was Père—I wish I was as good as Père Jerome."

"My child," said Madame Delphine, her tone betraying a painful summoning of strength to say what she had lacked the courage to utter,—"my child, I pray the good God you will not let your heart go after one whom you may never see in this world!"

The maiden turned her glance, and their eyes met. She cast her arms about her mother's neck, laid her cheek upon it for a moment, and then, feeling the maternal tear, lifted her lips, and, kissing her, said:

"I will not! I will not!"

But the voice was one, not of willing consent, but of desperate resolution.

"It would be useless, anyhow," said the mother, laying her arm around her daughter's waist.

Olive repeated the kiss, prolonging it passionately.

"I have nobody but you," murmured the girl; "I am a poor quadroone!"

She threw back her plaited hair for a third embrace, when a sound in the shrubbery startled them.

"Qui ci ça?" called Madame Delphine, in a frightened voice, as the two stood up, holding to each other.

No answer.

"It was only the dropping of a twig," she whispered, after a long holding of the breath. But they went into the house and barred it everywhere.

It was no longer pleasant to sit up. They retired, and in course of time, but not soon, they fell asleep, holding each other very tight, and fearing, even in their dreams, to hear another twig fall.

CHAPTER X

BIRDS

Monsieur Vignevielle looked in at no more doors or windows; but if the disappearance of this symptom was a favorable sign, others came to notice which were especially bad,—for instance, wakefulness. At well-nigh any hour of the night, the city guard, which itself dared not patrol singly, would meet him on his slow, unmolested, sky-gazing walk.

"Seems to enjoy it," said Jean Thompson; "the worst sort of evidence. If he showed distress of mind, it would not be so bad; but his calmness,—ugly feature."

The attorney had held his ground so long that he began really to believe it was tenable.

By day, it is true, Monsieur Vignevielle was at his post in his quiet "bank." Yet here, day by day, he was the source of more and more vivid astonishment to those who held preconceived notions of a banker's calling. As a banker, at least, he was certainly out of balance; while as a promenader, it seemed to those who watched him that his ruling idea had now veered about, and that of late he was ever on the quiet alert, not to find, but to evade, somebody.

"Olive, my child," whispered Madame Delphine one morning, as the pair were kneeling side by side on the tiled floor of the church, "yonder is Miché Vignevielle! If you will only look at once— he is just passing a little in——. Ah, much too slow again; he stepped out by the side door."

The mother thought it a strange providence that Monsieur Vignevielle should always be disappearing whenever Olive was with her.

One early dawn, Madame Delphine, with a small empty basket on her arm, stepped out upon the banquette in front of her house, shut and fastened the door very softly, and stole out in the direction whence you could faintly catch, in the stillness of the daybreak, the songs of the Gascon butchers and the pounding of their meat-axes on the stalls of the distant market-house. She was

34

going to see if she could find some birds for Olive,—the child's appetite was so poor; and, as she was out, she would drop an early prayer at the cathedral. Faith and works.

"One must venture something, sometimes, in the cause of religion," thought she, as she started timorously on her way. But she had not gone a dozen steps before she repented her temerity. There was some one behind her.

There should not be anything terrible in a footstep merely because it is masculine; but Madame Delphine's mind was not prepared to consider that. A terrible secret was haunting her. Yesterday morning she had found a shoe-track in the garden. She had not disclosed the discovery to Olive, but she had hardly closed her eyes the whole night.

The step behind her now might be the fall of that very shoe. She quickened her pace, but did not leave the sound behind. She hurried forward almost at a run; yet it was still there—no farther, no nearer. Two frights were upon her at once—one for herself, another for Olive, left alone in the house; but she had but the one prayer—"God protect my child!" After a fearful time she reached a place of safety, the cathedral. There, panting, she knelt long enough to know the pursuit was, at least, suspended, and then arose, hoping and praying all the saints that she might find the way clear for her return in all haste to Olive.

She approached a different door from that by which she had entered, her eyes in all directions and her heart in her throat.

"Madame Carraze."

She started wildly and almost screamed, though the voice was soft and mild. Monsieur Vignevielle came slowly forward from the shade of the wall. They met beside a bench, upon which she dropped her basket.

"Ah, Miché Vignevielle, I thang de good God to mid you!"

"Is dad so, Madame Carraze? Fo' w'y dad is?"

"A man was chase me all dad way since my 'ouse!"

"Yes, Madame, I sawed him."

"You sawed 'im? Oo it was?"

"'Twas only one man wad is a foolizh. De people say he's crezzie. Mais, he don' goin' to meg you no 'arm."

"But I was scare' fo' my lill' girl."

"Noboddie don' goin' trouble you' lill' gal, Madame Carraze."

Madame Delphine looked up into the speaker's strangely kind and patient eyes, and drew sweet re-assurance from them.

"Madame," said Monsieur Vignevielle, "wad pud you hout so hearly dis morning?"

She told him her errand. She asked if he thought she would find anything.

"Yez," he said, "it was possible—a few lill' bécassines-de-mer, ou somezin' ligue. But fo' w'y you lill' gal lose doze hapetide?"

"Ah, Miché,"—Madame Delphine might have tried a thousand times again without ever succeeding half so well in lifting the curtain upon the whole, sweet, tender, old, old-fashioned truth,— "Ah, Miché, she wone tell me!"

"Bud, anny'ow, Madame, wad you thing?"

"Miché," she replied, looking up again with a tear standing in either eye, and then looking down once more as she began to speak, "I thing—I thing she's lonesome."

"You thing?"

She nodded.

"Ah! Madame Carraze," he said, partly extending his hand, "you see? 'Tis impossible to mague you' owze shud so tighd to priv-en dad. Madame, I med one mizteg."

"Ah, non, Miché!"

"Yez. There har nod one poss'bil'ty fo' me to be dad guardian of you' daughteh!"

Madame Delphine started with surprise and alarm.

"There is ondly one wad can be," he continued.

"But oo, Miché?"

"God."

"Ah, Miché Vignevielle——" She looked at him appealingly.

"I don' goin' to dizzerd you, Madame Carraze," he said.

She lifted her eyes. They filled. She shook her head, a tear fell, she bit her lip, smiled, and suddenly dropped her face into both hands, sat down upon the bench and wept until she shook.

"You dunno wad I mean, Madame Carraze?"

She did not know.

"I mean dad guardian of you' daughteh godd to fine 'er now one 'uzban'; an' noboddie are hable to do dad egceb de good God 'imsev. But, Madame, I tell you wad I do."

She rose up. He continued:

"Go h-open you' owze; I fin' you' daughteh dad' uzban'."

Madame Delphine was a helpless, timid thing; but her eyes showed she was about to resent this offer. Monsieur Vignevielle put forth his hand—it touched her shoulder—and said, kindly still, and without eagerness.

"One w'ite man, Madame; 'tis prattycabble. I know 'tis prattycabble. One w'ite jantleman, Madame. You can truz me. I goin' fedge 'im. H-ondly you go h-open you' owze."

Madame Delphine looked down, twining her handkerchief among her fingers.

He repeated his proposition.

"You will come firz by you'se'f?" she asked.

"Iv you wand."

She lifted up once more her eye of faith. That was her answer.

"Come," he said, gently, "I wan' sen' some bird ad you' lill' gal."

And they went away, Madame Delphine's spirit grown so exaltedly bold that she said as they went, though a violent blush followed her words:

"Miché Vignevielle, I thing Père Jerome mighd be ab'e to tell you someboddie."

CHAPTER XI

FACE TO FACE

Madame Delphine found her house neither burned nor rifled.

"Ah! ma piti sans popa! Ah! my little fatherless one!" Her faded bonnet fell back between her shoulders, hanging on by the strings, and her dropped basket, with its "few lill' bécassines-de-mer" dangling from the handle, rolled out its okra and soup-joint upon the floor. "Ma piti! kiss!—kiss!—kiss!"

"But is it good news you have, or bad?" cried the girl, a fourth or fifth time.

"Dieu sait, ma c'ère; mo pas conné!"—God knows, my darling; I cannot tell!

The mother dropped into a chair, covered her face with her apron, and burst into tears, then looked up with an effort to smile, and wept afresh.

"What have you been doing?" asked the daughter, in a long-drawn, fondling tone. She leaned forward and unfastened her mother's bonnet-strings. "Why do you cry?"

"For nothing at all, my darling; for nothing—I am such a fool."

The girl's eyes filled. The mother looked up into her face and said:

"No, it is nothing, nothing, only that—" turning her head from side to side with a slow, emotional emphasis, "Miché Vignevielle is the best—best man on the good Lord's earth!"

Olive drew a chair close to her mother, sat down and took the little yellow hands into her own white lap, and looked tenderly into her eyes. Madame Delphine felt herself yielding; she must make a show of telling something:

"He sent you those birds!"

The girl drew her face back a little. The little woman turned away, trying in vain to hide her tearful smile, and they laughed together, Olive mingling a daughter's fond kiss with her laughter.

"There is something else," she said, "and you shall tell me."

"Yes," replied Madame Delphine, "only let me get composed."

But she did not get so. Later in the morning she came to Olive with the timid yet startling proposal that they would do what they could to brighten up the long-neglected front room. Olive was mystified and troubled, but consented, and thereupon the mother's spirits rose.

The work began, and presently ensued all the thumping, the trundling, the lifting and letting down, the raising and swallowing of dust, and the smells of turpentine, brass, pumice and woollen rags that go to characterize a housekeeper's émeute; and still, as the work progressed, Madame Delphine's heart grew light, and her little black eyes sparkled.

"We like a clean parlor, my daughter, even though no one is ever coming to see us, eh?" she said, as entering the apartment she at last sat down, late in the afternoon. She had put on her best attire.

Olive was not there to reply. The mother called but got no answer. She rose with an uneasy heart, and met her a few steps beyond the door that opened into the garden, in a path which came up from an old latticed bower. Olive was approaching slowly, her face pale and wild. There was an agony of hostile dismay in the look, and the trembling and appealing tone with which, taking the frightened mother's cheeks between her palms, she said:

"Ah! ma mère, qui vini 'ci ce soir?"—Who is coming here this evening?

"Why, my dear child, I was just saying, we like a clean——"

But the daughter was desperate:

"Oh, tell me, my mother, who is coming?"

"My darling, it is our blessed friend, Miché Vignevielle!"

"To see me?" cried the girl.

"Yes."

"Oh, my mother, what have you done?"

"Why, Olive, my child," exclaimed the little mother, bursting into tears, "do you forget it is Miché Vignevielle who has promised to protect you when I die?"

The daughter had turned away, and entered the door; but she faced around again, and extending her arms toward her mother, cried:

"How can—he is a white man—I am a poor——"

"Ah! chérie" replied Madame Delphine, seizing the outstretched hands, "it is there—it is there that he shows himself the best man alive! He sees that difficulty; he proposes to meet it; he says he will find you a suitor!"

Olive freed her hands violently, motioned her mother back,

39

and stood proudly drawn up, flashing an indignation too great for speech; but the next moment she had uttered a cry, and was sobbing on the floor.

The mother knelt beside her and threw an arm about her shoulders.

"Oh, my sweet daughter, you must not cry! I did not want to tell you at all! I did not want to tell you! It isn't fair for you to cry so hard. Miché Vignevielle says you shall have the one you wish, or none at all, Olive, or none at all."

"None at all! none at all! None, none, none!"

"No, no, Olive," said the mother, "none at all. He brings none with him to-night, and shall bring none with him hereafter."

Olive rose suddenly, silently declined her mother's aid, and went alone to their chamber in the half-story.

Madame Delphine wandered drearily from door to window, from window to door, and presently into the newly-furnished front room which now seemed dismal beyond degree. There was a great Argand lamp in one corner. How she had labored that day to prepare it for evening illumination! A little beyond it, on the wall, hung a crucifix. She knelt under it, with her eyes fixed upon it, and thus silently remained until its outline was undistinguishable in the deepening shadows of evening.

She arose. A few minutes later, as she was trying to light the lamp, an approaching step on the sidewalk seemed to pause. Her heart stood still. She softly laid the phosphorus-box out of her hands. A shoe grated softly on the stone step, and Madame Delphine, her heart beating in great thuds, without waiting for a knock, opened the door, bowed low, and exclaimed in a soft perturbed voice:

"Miché Vignevielle!"

He entered, hat in hand, and with that almost noiseless tread which we have noticed. She gave him a chair and closed the door; then hastened, with words of apology, back to her task of lighting the lamp. But her hands paused in their work again,—Olive's step was on the stairs; then it came off the stairs; then it was in the next room, and then there was the whisper of soft robes, a breath of gentle perfume, and a snowy figure in the door. She was dressed for the evening.

"Maman?"

Madame Delphine was struggling desperately with the lamp, and at that moment it responded with a tiny bead of light.

"I am here, my daughter."

She hastened to the door, and Olive, all unaware of a third

presence, lifted her white arms, laid them about her mother's neck, and, ignoring her effort to speak, wrested a fervent kiss from her lips. The crystal of the lamp sent out a faint gleam; it grew; it spread on every side; the ceiling, the walls lighted up; the crucifix, the furniture of the room came back into shape.

"Maman!" cried Olive, with a tremor of consternation.

"It is Miché Vignevielle, my daughter——"

The gloom melted swiftly away before the eyes of the startled maiden, a dark form stood out against the farther wall, and the light, expanding to the full, shone clearly upon the unmoving figure and quiet face of Capitaine Lemaitre.

CHAPTER XII

THE MOTHER BIRD

One afternoon, some three weeks after Capitaine Lemaitre had called on Madame Delphine, the priest started to make a pastoral call and had hardly left the gate of his cottage, when a person, overtaking him, plucked his gown:

"Père Jerome——"

He turned.

The face that met his was so changed with excitement and distress that for an instant he did not recognize it.

"Why, Madame Delphine——"

"Oh, Père Jerome! I wan' see you so bad, so bad! Mo oulé dit quiç'ose,—I godd some' to tell you."

The two languages might be more successful than one, she seemed to think.

"We had better go back to my parlor," said the priest, in their native tongue.

They returned.

Madame Delphine's very step was altered,—nervous and inelastic. She swung one arm as she walked, and brandished a turkey-tail fan.

"I was glad, yass, to kedge you," she said, as they mounted the front, outdoor stair; following her speech with a slight, unmusical laugh, and fanning herself with unconscious fury.

"Fé chaud," she remarked again, taking the chair he offered and continuing to ply the fan.

Père Jerome laid his hat upon a chest of drawers, sat down opposite her, and said, as he wiped his kindly face:

"Well, Madame Carraze?"

Gentle as the tone was, she started, ceased fanning, lowered the fan to her knee, and commenced smoothing its feathers.

"Père Jerome——" She gnawed her lip and shook her head.

"Well?"

She burst into tears.

42

The priest rose and loosed the curtain of one of the windows. He did it slowly—as slowly as he could, and, as he came back, she lifted her face with sudden energy, and exclaimed:

"Oh, Père Jerome, de law is brogue! de law is brogue! I brogue it! 'Twas me! 'Twas me!"

The tears gushed out again, but she shut her lips very tight, and dumbly turned away her face. Père Jerome waited a little before replying; then he said, very gently:

"I suppose dad muss 'ave been by accyden', Madame Delphine?"

The little father felt a wish—one which he often had when weeping women were before him—that he were an angel instead of a man, long enough to press the tearful cheek upon his breast, and assure the weeper God would not let the lawyers and judges hurt her. He allowed a few moments more to pass, and then asked:

"N'est-ce-pas, Madame Delphine? Daz ze way, aint it?"

"No, Père Jerome, no. My daughter—oh, Père Jerome, I bethroath my lill' girl—to a w'ite man!" And immediately Madame Delphine commenced savagely drawing a thread in the fabric of her skirt with one trembling hand, while she drove the fan with the other. "Dey goin' git marry."

On the priest's face came a look of pained surprise. He slowly said:

"Is dad possib', Madame Delphine?"

"Yass," she replied, at first without lifting her eyes; and then again, "Yass," looking full upon him through her tears, "yass, 'tis tru'."

He rose and walked once across the room, returned, and said, in the Creole dialect:

"Is he a good man—without doubt?"

"De bez in God's world!" replied Madame Delphine, with a rapturous smile.

"My poor, dear friend," said the priest, "I am afraid you are being deceived by somebody."

There was the pride of an unswerving faith in the triumphant tone and smile with which she replied, raising and slowly shaking her head:

"Ah-h, no-o-o, Miché! Ah-h, no, no! Not by Ursin Lemaitre-Vignevielle!"

Père Jerome was confounded. He turned again, and, with his hands at his back and his eyes cast down, slowly paced the floor.

"He is a good man," he said, by and by, as if he thought aloud. At length he halted before the woman.

"Madame Delphine——"

43

The distressed glance with which she had been following his steps was lifted to his eyes.

"Suppose dad should be true w'at doze peop' say 'bout Ursin."

"Qui ci ça? What is that?" asked the quadroone, stopping her fan.

"Some peop' say Ursin is crezzie."

"Ah, Père Jerome!" She leaped to her feet as if he had smitten her, and putting his words away with an outstretched arm and wide-open palm, suddenly lifted hands and eyes to heaven, and cried: "I wizh to God—I wizh to God—de whole worl' was crezzie dad same way!" She sank, trembling, into her chair. "Oh, no, no," she continued, shaking her head, "'tis not Miché Vignevielle w'at's crezzie." Her eyes lighted with sudden fierceness. "'Tis dad law! Dad law is crezzie! Dad law is a fool!"

A priest of less heart-wisdom might have replied that the law is—the law; but Père Jerome saw that Madame Delphine was expecting this very response. Wherefore he said, with gentleness:

"Madame Delphine, a priest is not a bailiff, but a physician. How can I help you?"

A grateful light shone a moment in her eyes, yet there remained a piteous hostility in the tone in which she demanded:

"Mais, pou'quoi yé fé cette méchanique là?"—What business had they to make that contraption?

His answer was a shrug with his palms extended and a short, disclamatory "Ah." He started to resume his walk, but turned to her again and said:

"Why did they make that law? Well, they made it to keep the two races separate."

Madame Delphine startled the speaker with a loud, harsh, angry laugh. Fire came from her eyes and her lip curled with scorn.

"Then they made a lie, Père Jerome! Separate! No-o-o! They do not want to keep us separated; no, no! But they do want to keep us despised!" She laid her hand on her heart, and frowned upward with physical pain. "But, very well! from which race do they want to keep my daughter separate? She is seven parts white! The law did not stop her from being that; and now, when she wants to be a white man's good and honest wife, shall that law stop her? Oh, no!" She rose up. "No; I will tell you what that law is made for. It is made to—punish—my—child—for—not—choosing—her—father! Père Jerome—my God, what a law!" She dropped back into her seat. The tears came in a flood, which she made no attempt to restrain.

"No," she began again—and here she broke into English—"fo' me I don' kyare; but, Père Jerome,—'tis fo' dat I come to tell you,—dey shall not punizh my daughter!" She was on her feet again,

44

smiting her heaving bosom with the fan. "She shall marrie oo she want!"

Père Jerome had heard her out, not interrupting by so much as a motion of the hand. Now his decision was made, and he touched her softly with the ends of his fingers.

"Madame Delphine, I want you to go at 'ome. Go at 'ome."

"Wad you goin' mague?" she asked.

"Nottin'. But go at 'ome. Kip quite; don' put you'se'f sig. I goin' see Ursin. We trah to figs dat law fo' you."

"You kin figs dad!" she cried, with a gleam of joy.

"We goin' to try, Madame Delphine. Adieu!"

He offered his hand. She seized and kissed it thrice, covering it with tears, at the same time lifting up her eyes to his and murmuring:

"De bez man God evva mague!"

At the door she turned to offer a more conventional good-bye; but he was following her out, bareheaded. At the gate they paused an instant, and then parted with a simple adieu, she going home and he returning for his hat, and starting again upon his interrupted business.

Before he came back to his own house, he stopped at the lodgings of Monsieur Vignevielle, but did not find him in.

"Indeed," the servant at the door said, "he said he might not return for some days or weeks."

So Père Jerome, much wondering, made a second detour toward the residence of one of Monsieur Vignevielle's employés.

"Yes," said the clerk, "his instructions are to hold the business, as far as practicable, in suspense, during his absence. Everything is in another name." And then he whispered:

"Officers of the Government looking for him. Information got from some of the prisoners taken months ago by the United States brig Porpoise. But"—a still softer whisper—"have no fear; they will never find him: Jean Thompson and Evariste Varrillat have hid him away too well for that."

CHAPTER XIII

TRIBULATION

The Saturday following was a very beautiful day. In the morning a light fall of rain had passed across the town, and all the afternoon you could see signs, here and there upon the horizon, of other showers. The ground was dry again, while the breeze was cool and sweet, smelling of wet foliage and bringing sunshine and shade in frequent and very pleasing alternation.

There was a walk in Père Jerome's little garden, of which we have not spoken, off on the right side of the cottage, with his chamber window at one end, a few old and twisted, but blossom-laden, crape-myrtles on either hand, now and then a rose of some unpretending variety and some bunches of rue, and at the other end a shrine, in whose blue niche stood a small figure of Mary, with folded hands and uplifted eyes. No other window looked down upon the spot, and its seclusion was often a great comfort to Père Jerome.

Up and down this path, but a few steps in its entire length, the priest was walking, taking the air for a few moments after a prolonged sitting in the confessional. Penitents had been numerous this afternoon. He was thinking of Ursin. The officers of the Government had not found him, nor had Père Jerome seen him; yet he believed they had, in a certain indirect way, devised a simple project by which they could at any time "figs dad law," providing only that these Government officials would give over their search; for, though he had not seen the fugitive, Madame Delphine had seen him, and had been the vehicle of communication between them. There was an orange-tree, where a mocking-bird was wont to sing and a girl in white to walk, that the detectives wot not of. The law was to be "figs" by the departure of the three frequenters of the jasmine-scented garden in one ship to France, where the law offered no obstacles.

It seemed moderately certain to those in search of Monsieur Vignevielle (and it was true) that Jean and Evariste were his harborers; but for all that the hunt, even for clues, was vain. The little banking establishment had not been disturbed. Jean Thompson had told the searchers certain facts about it, and about its gentle proprietor as well, that persuaded them to make no move against the concern, if the same relations did not even induce a relaxation of their efforts for his personal discovery.

Père Jerome was walking to and fro, with his hands behind him, pondering these matters. He had paused a moment at the end of the walk furthest from his window, and was looking around upon the sky, when, turning, he beheld a closely veiled female figure standing at the other end, and knew instantly that it was Olive.

She came forward quickly and with evident eagerness.

"I came to confession," she said, breathing hurriedly, the excitement in her eyes shining through her veil, "but I find I am too late."

"There is no too late or too early for that; I am always ready," said the priest. "But how is your mother?"

"Ah!——"

Her voice failed.

"More trouble?"

"Ah, sir, I have made trouble. Oh, Père Jerome, I am bringing so much trouble upon my poor mother!"

Père Jerome moved slowly toward the house, with his eyes cast down, the veiled girl at his side.

"It is not your fault," he presently said. And after another pause: "I thought it was all arranged."

He looked up and could see, even through the veil, her crimson blush.

"Oh, no," she replied, in a low, despairing voice, dropping her face.

"What is the difficulty?" asked the priest, stopping in the angle of the path, where it turned toward the front of the house.

She averted her face, and began picking the thin scales of bark from a crape-myrtle.

"Madame Thompson and her husband were at our house this morning. He had told Monsieur Thompson all about it. They were very kind to me at first, but they tried——" She was weeping.

"What did they try to do?" asked the priest.

"They tried to make me believe he is insane."

She succeeded in passing her handkerchief up under her veil.

"And I suppose then your poor mother grew angry, eh?"

"Yes; and they became much more so, and said if we did not write, or send a writing, to him, within twenty-four hours, breaking the——"

"Engagement," said Père Jerome.

"They would give him up to the Government. Oh, Père Jerome, what shall I do? It is killing my mother!"

She bowed her head and sobbed.

"Where is your mother now?"

"She has gone to see Monsieur Jean Thompson. She says she has a plan that will match them all. I do not know what it is. I begged her not to go; but oh, sir, she is crazy,—and—I am no better."

"My poor child," said Père Jerome, "what you seem to want is not absolution, but relief from persecution."

"Oh, father, I have committed mortal sin,—I am guilty of pride and anger."

"Nevertheless," said the priest, starting toward his front gate, "we will put off your confession. Let it go until to-morrow morning; you will find me in my box just before mass; I will hear you then. My child, I know that in your heart, now, you begrudge the time it would take; and that is right. There are moments when we are not in place even on penitential knees. It is so with you now. We must find your mother. Go you at once to your house; if she is there, comfort her as best you can, and keep her in, if possible, until I come. If she is not there, stay; leave me to find her; one of you, at least, must be where I can get word to you promptly. God comfort and uphold you. I hope you may find her at home; tell her, for me, not to fear,"—he lifted the gate-latch,—"that she and her daughter are of more value than many sparrows; that God's priest sends her that word from Him. Tell her to fix her trust in the great Husband of the Church, and she shall yet see her child receiving the grace-giving sacrament of matrimony. Go; I shall, in a few minutes, be on my way to Jean Thompson's, and shall find her, either there or wherever she is. Go; they shall not oppress you. Adieu!"

A moment or two later he was in the street himself.

CHAPTER XIV

BY AN OATH

Père Jerome, pausing on a street-corner in the last hour of sunlight, had wiped his brow and taken his cane down from under his arm to start again, when somebody, coming noiselessly from he knew not where, asked, so suddenly as to startle him:

"Miché, commin yé 'pellé la rie ici?—how do they call this street here?"

It was by the bonnet and dress, disordered though they were, rather than by the haggard face which looked distractedly around, that he recognized the woman to whom he replied in her own patois:

"It is the Rue Burgundy. Where are you going, Madame Delphine?"

She almost leaped from the ground.

"Oh, Père Jerome! mo pas conné,—I dunno. You know w'ere's dad 'ouse of Michè Jean Tomkin? Mo courri 'ci, mo courri là,—mo pas capale li trouvé. I go (run) here—there—I cannot find it," she gesticulated.

"I am going there myself," said he; "but why do you want to see Jean Thompson, Madame Delphine?"

"I 'blige' to see 'im!" she replied, jerking herself half around away, one foot planted forward with an air of excited preoccupation; "I god some' to tell 'im wad I 'blige' to tell 'im!"

"Madame Delphine——"

"Oh! Père Jerome, fo' de love of de good God, show me dad way to de 'ouse of Jean Tomkin!"

Her distressed smile implored pardon for her rudeness.

"What are you going to tell him?" asked the priest.

"Oh, Père Jerome,"—in the Creole patois again,—"I am going to put an end to all this trouble—only I pray you do not ask me about it now; every minute is precious!"

He could not withstand her look of entreaty.

"Come," he said, and they went.

49

Jean Thompson and Doctor Varrillat lived opposite each other on the Bayou road, a little way beyond the town limits as then prescribed. Each had his large, white-columned, four-sided house among the magnolias,—his huge live-oak overshadowing either corner of the darkly shaded garden, his broad, brick walk leading down to the tall, brick-pillared gate, his square of bright, red pavement on the turf-covered sidewalk, and his railed platform spanning the draining-ditch, with a pair of green benches, one on each edge, facing each other crosswise of the gutter. There, any sunset hour, you were sure to find the householder sitting beside his cool-robed matron, two or three slave nurses in white turbans standing at hand, and an excited throng of fair children, nearly all of a size.

Sometimes, at a beckon or call, the parents on one side of the way would join those on the other, and the children and nurses of both families would be given the liberty of the opposite platform and an ice-cream fund! Generally the parents chose the Thompson platform, its outlook being more toward the sunset.

Such happened to be the arrangement this afternoon. The two husbands sat on one bench and their wives on the other, both pairs very quiet, waiting respectfully for the day to die, and exchanging only occasional comments on matters of light moment as they passed through the memory. During one term of silence Madame Varrillat, a pale, thin-faced, but cheerful-looking lady, touched Madame Thompson, a person of two and a half times her weight, on her extensive and snowy bare elbow, directing her attention obliquely up and across the road.

About a hundred yards distant, in the direction of the river, was a long, pleasantly shaded green strip of turf, destined in time for a sidewalk. It had a deep ditch on the nearer side, and a fence of rough cypress palisades on the farther, and these were overhung, on the one hand, by a row of bitter orange-trees inside the inclosure, and, on the other, by a line of slanting china-trees along the outer edge of the ditch. Down this cool avenue two figures were approaching side by side. They had first attracted Madame Varrillat's notice by the bright play of sunbeams which, as they walked, fell upon them in soft, golden flashes through the chinks between the palisades.

Madame Thompson elevated a pair of glasses which were no detraction from her very good looks, and remarked, with the serenity of a reconnoitering general:

"Père Jerome et cette milatraise."

All eyes were bent toward them.

"She walks like a man," said Madame Varrillat, in the language with which the conversation had opened.

"No," said the physician, "like a woman in a state of high nervous excitement."

Jean Thompson kept his eyes on the woman, and said:

"She must not forget to walk like a woman in the State of Louisiana,"—as near as the pun can be translated. The company laughed. Jean Thompson looked at his wife, whose applause he prized, and she answered by an asseverative toss of the head, leaning back and contriving, with some effort, to get her arms folded. Her laugh was musical and low, but enough to make the folded arms shake gently up and down.

"Père Jerome is talking to her," said one. The priest was at that moment endeavoring, in the interest of peace, to say a good word for the four people who sat watching his approach. It was in the old strain:

"Blame them one part, Madame Delphine, and their fathers, mothers, brothers, and fellow-citizens the other ninety-nine."

But to everything she had the one amiable answer which Père Jerome ignored:

"I am going to arrange it to satisfy everybody, all together. Tout à fait."

"They are coming here," said Madame Varrillat, half articulately.

"Well, of course," murmured another; and the four rose up, smiling courteously, the doctor and attorney advancing and shaking hands with the priest.

No—Père Jerome thanked them—he could not sit down.

"This, I believe you know, Jean, is Madame Delphine——"

The quadroone curtsied.

"A friend of mine," he added, smiling kindly upon her, and turning, with something imperative in his eye, to the group. "She says she has an important private matter to communicate."

"To me?" asked Jean Thompson.

"To all of you; so I will—— Good-evening." He responded nothing to the expressions of regret, but turned to Madame Delphine. She murmured something.

"Ah! yes, certainly." He addressed the company: "She wishes me to speak for her veracity; it is unimpeachable. "Well, good-evening." He shook hands and departed.

The four resumed their seats, and turned their eyes upon the standing figure.

"Have you something to say to us?" asked Jean Thompson, frowning at her law-defying bonnet.

"Oui," replied the woman, shrinking to one side, and laying hold of one of the benches, "mo oulé di' tou' ç'ose"—I want to tell everything. "Miché Vignevielle la plis bon homme di moune"—the best man in the world; "mo pas capabe li fé tracas"—I cannot give him trouble. "Mo pas capabe, non; m'olé di' tous ç'ose." She attempted to fan herself, her face turned away from the attorney, and her eyes rested on the ground.

"Take a seat," said Doctor Varrillat, with some suddenness, starting from his place and gently guiding her sinking form into the corner of the bench. The ladies rose up; somebody had to stand; the two races could not both sit down at once—at least not in that public manner.

"Your salts," said the physician to his wife. She handed the vial. Madame Delphine stood up again.

"We will all go inside," said Madame Thompson, and they passed through the gate and up the walk, mounted the steps, and entered the deep, cool drawing-room.

Madame Thompson herself bade the quadroone be seated.

"Well?" said Jean Thompson, as the rest took chairs.

"C'est drole"—it's funny—said Madame Delphine, with a piteous effort to smile, "that nobody thought of it. It is so plain. You have only to look and see. I mean about Olive." She loosed a button in the front of her dress and passed her hand into her bosom. "And yet, Olive herself never thought of it. She does not know a word."

The hand came out holding a miniature. Madame Varrillat passed it to Jean Thompson.

"Ouala so popa" said Madame Delphine. "That is her father."

It went from one to another, exciting admiration and murmured praise.

"She is the image of him," said Madame Thompson, in an austere under-tone, returning it to her husband.

Doctor Varrillat was watching Madame Delphine. She was very pale. She had passed a trembling hand into a pocket of her skirt, and now drew out another picture, in a case the counterpart of the first. He reached out for it, and she handed it to him. He looked at it a moment, when his eyes suddenly lighted up and he passed it to the attorney.

"Et là"—Madame Delphine's utterance failed—"et là, ouala sa moman." (That is her mother.)

The three others instantly gathered around Jean Thompson's chair. They were much impressed.

"It is true beyond a doubt!" muttered Madame Thompson.

Madame Varrillat looked at her with astonishment.

"The proof is right there in the faces," said Madame Thompson.

"Yes! yes!" said Madame Delphine, excitedly; "the proof is there! You do not want any better! I am willing to swear to it! But you want no better proof! That is all anybody could want! My God! you cannot help but see it!"

Her manner was wild.

Jean Thompson looked at her sternly.

"Nevertheless you say you are willing to take your solemn oath to this."

"Certainly——"

"You will have to do it."

"Certainly, Miché Thompson, of course I shall; you will make out the paper and I will swear before God that it is true! Only"—turning to the ladies—"do not tell Olive; she will never believe it. It will break her heart! It——"

A servant came and spoke privately to Madame Thompson, who rose quickly and went to the hall. Madame Delphine continued, rising unconsciously:

"You see, I have had her with me from a baby. She knows no better. He brought her to me only two months old. Her mother had died in the ship, coming out here. He did not come straight from home here. His people never knew he was married!"

The speaker looked around suddenly with a startled glance. There was a noise of excited speaking in the hall.

"It is not true, Madame Thompson!" cried a girl's voice.

Madame Delphine's look became one of wildest distress and alarm, and she opened her lips in a vain attempt to utter some request, when Olive appeared a moment in the door, and then flew into her arms.

"My mother! my mother! my mother!"

Madame Thompson, with tears in her eyes, tenderly drew them apart and let Madame Delphine down into her chair, while Olive threw herself upon her knees, continuing to cry:

"Oh, my mother! Say you are my mother!"

Madame Delphine looked an instant into the upturned face, and then turned her own away, with a long, low cry of pain, looked again, and laying both hands upon the suppliant's head, said:

"Oh, chère piti à moin, to pa' ma fie!" (Oh, my darling little one, you are not my daughter!) Her eyes closed, and her head sank back; the two gentlemen sprang to her assistance, and laid her upon a sofa unconscious.

When they brought her to herself, Olive was kneeling at her head silently weeping.

"Maman, chère maman!" said the girl softly, kissing her lips.

"Ma courri c'ez moin" (I will go home), said the mother, drearily.

"You will go home with me," said Madame Varrillat, with great kindness of manner—"just across the street here; I will take care of you till you feel better. And Olive will stay here with Madame Thompson. You will be only the width of the street apart."

But Madame Delphine would go nowhere but to her home. Olive she would not allow to go with her. Then they wanted to send a servant or two to sleep in the house with her for aid and protection; but all she would accept was the transient service of a messenger to invite two of her kinspeople—man and wife—to come and make their dwelling with her.

In course of time these two—a poor, timid, helpless, pair—fell heir to the premises. Their children had it after them; but, whether in those hands or these, the house had its habits and continued in them; and to this day the neighbors, as has already been said, rightly explain its close-sealed, uninhabited look by the all-sufficient statement that the inmates "is quadroons."

CHAPTER XV

KYRIE ELEISON

The second Saturday afternoon following was hot and calm. The lamp burning before the tabernacle in Père Jerome's little church might have hung with as motionless a flame in the window behind. The lilies of St. Joseph's wand, shining in one of the half opened panes, were not more completely at rest than the leaves on tree and vine without, suspended in the slumbering air. Almost as still, down under the organ-gallery, with a single band of light falling athwart his box from a small door which stood ajar, sat the little priest, behind the lattice of the confessional, silently wiping away the sweat that beaded on his brow and rolled down his face. At distant intervals the shadow of some one entering softly through the door would obscure, for a moment, the band of light, and an aged crone, or a little boy, or some gentle presence that the listening confessor had known only by the voice for many years, would kneel a few moments beside his waiting ear, in prayer for blessing and in review of those slips and errors which prove us all akin.

The day had been long and fatiguing. First, early mass; a hasty meal; then a business call upon the archbishop in the interest of some projected charity; then back to his cottage, and so to the banking-house of "Vignevielle," in the Rue Toulouse. There all was open, bright, and re-assured, its master virtually, though not actually, present. The search was over and the seekers gone, personally wiser than they would tell, and officially reporting that (to the best of their knowledge and belief, based on evidence, and especially on the assurances of an unexceptionable eyewitness, to wit, Monsieur Vignevielle, banker) Capitaine Lemaitre was dead and buried. At noon there had been a wedding in the little church. Its scenes lingered before Père Jerome's vision now—the kneeling pair: the bridegroom, rich in all the excellences of man, strength and kindness slumbering interlocked in every part and feature; the bride, a saintly weariness on her pale face, her awesome eyes lifted in adoration upon the image of the Saviour; the small knots of

55

friends behind: Madame Thompson, large, fair, self-contained; Jean Thompson, with the affidavit of Madame Delphine showing through his tightly buttoned coat; the physician and his wife, sharing one expression of amiable consent; and last—yet first—one small, shrinking female figure, here at one side, in faded robes and dingy bonnet. She sat as motionless as stone, yet wore a look of apprehension, and in the small, restless black eyes which peered out from the pinched and wasted face, betrayed the peacelessness of a harrowed mind; and neither the recollection of bride, nor of groom, nor of potential friends behind, nor the occupation of the present hour, could shut out from the tired priest the image of that woman, or the sound of his own low words of invitation to her, given as the company left the church—"Come to confession this afternoon."

By and by a long time passed without the approach of any step, or any glancing of light or shadow, save for the occasional progress from station to station of some one over on the right who was noiselessly going the way of the cross. Yet Père Jerome tarried.

"She will surely come," he said to himself; "she promised she would come."

A moment later, his sense, quickened by the prolonged silence, caught a subtle evidence or two of approach, and the next moment a penitent knelt noiselessly at the window of his box, and the whisper came tremblingly, in the voice he had waited to hear:

"Bénissez-moin, mo' Père, pa'ce que mo péché." (Bless me, father, for I have sinned.)

He gave his blessing.

"Ainsi soit-il—Amen," murmured the penitent, and then, in the soft accents of the Creole patois, continued:

"'I confess to Almighty God, to the blessed Mary, ever Virgin, to blessed Michael the Archangel, to blessed John the Baptist, to the holy Apostles Peter and Paul, and to all the saints, that I have sinned exceedingly in thought, word, and deed, through my fault, through my fault, through my most grievous fault.' I confessed on Saturday, three weeks ago, and received absolution, and I have performed the penance enjoined. Since then——" There she stopped.

There was a soft stir, as if she sank slowly down, and another as if she rose up again, and in a moment she said:

"Olive is my child. The picture I showed to Jean Thompson is the half-sister of my daughter's father, dead before my child was born. She is the image of her and of him; but, O God! Thou knowest! Oh Olive, my own daughter!"

She ceased, and was still. Père Jerome waited, but no sound

came. He looked through the window. She was kneeling, with her forehead resting on her arms—motionless.

He repeated the words of absolution. Still she did not stir.

"My daughter," he said, "go to thy home in peace." But she did not move.

He rose hastily, stepped from the box, raised her in his arms, and called her by name:

"Madame Delphine!" Her head fell back in his elbow; for an instant there was life in the eyes—it glimmered—it vanished, and tears gushed from his own and fell upon the gentle face of the dead, as he looked up to heaven and cried:

"Lord, lay not this sin to her charge!"

BYLOW HILL

I

RUTH AND GODFREY

The old street, keeping its New England Sabbath afternoon so decently under its majestic elms, was as goodly an example of its sort as the late seventies of the century just gone could show. It lay along a north-and-south ridge, between a number of aged and unsmiling cottages, fronting on cinder sidewalks, and alternating irregularly with about as many larger homesteads that sat back in their well-shaded gardens with kindlier dignity and not so grim a self-assertion. Behind, on the west, these gardens dropped swiftly out of sight to a hidden brook, from the farther shore of which rose the great wooded hill whose shelter from the bitter northwest had invited the old Puritan founders to choose the spot for their farming village of one street, with a Byington and a Winslow for their first town officers. In front, eastward, the land declined gently for a half mile or so, covered, by modern prosperity, with a small, stanch town, and bordered by a pretty river winding among meadows of hay and grain. At the northern end, instead of this gentle decline, was a precipitous cliff side, close to whose brow a wooden bench, that ran half-way round a vast sidewalk tree, commanded a view of the valley embracing nearly three-quarters of the compass.

In civilian's dress, and with only his sea-bronzed face and the polished air of a pivot gun to tell that he was of the navy, Lieutenant Godfrey Winslow was slowly crossing the rural way with Ruth Byington at his side. He had the look of, say, twenty-eight, and she was some four years his junior. From her father's front gate they were passing toward the large grove garden of the young man's own home, on the side next the hill and the sunset. On the front porch, where the two had just left him, sat the war-crippled father of the girl, taking pride in the placidity of the face she once or twice turned to him in profile, and in the buoyancy of her movements and pose.

His fond, unspoken thought went after her, that she was hiding some care again,—her old, sweet trick, and her mother's before her.

He looked on to Godfrey. "There's endurance," he thought again. "You ought to have taken him long ago, my good girl, if you want him at all." And here his reflections faded into the unworded belief that she would have done so but for his, her own father's, being in the way.

The pair stopped and turned half about to enjoy the green-arched vista of the street, and Godfrey said, in a tone that left his companion no room to overlook its personal intent, "How often, in my long absences, I see this spot!"

"You wouldn't dare confess you didn't," was her blithe reply.

"Oh yes, I should. I've tried not to see it, many a time."

"Why, Godfrey Winslow!" she laughed. "That was very wrong!"

"It was very useless," said the wanderer, "for there was always the same one girl in the midst of the picture; and that's the sort a man can never shut out, you know. I don't try to shut it out any more, Ruth."

The girl spoke more softly. "I wish I could know where Leonard is," she mused aloud.

"Did you hear me, Ruth? I say I don't try any more, now."

"Well, that's right! I wonder where that brother of mine is?"

The baffled lover had to call up his patience. "Well, that's right, too," he laughed; "and I wonder where that brother of mine is? I wonder if they're together?"

They moved on, but at the stately entrance of the Winslow garden they paused again. The girl gave her companion a look of distress, and the young man's brow darkened. "Say it," he said. "I see what it is."

"You speak of Arthur"—she began.

"Well?"

"What did you make out of his sermon this morning?"

"Why, Ruth, I—What did you make out of it?"

"I made out that the poor boy is very, very unhappy."

"Did you? Well, he is; and in a certain way I'm to blame for it."

The girl's smile was tender. "Was there ever anything the matter with Arthur, and you didn't think you were in some way to blame for it?"

59

"Oh, now, don't confuse me with Leonard. Anyhow, I'm to blame this time! Has Isabel told you anything, Ruth?"

"Yes, Isabel has told me!"

"Told you they are engaged?"

"Told me they are engaged!"

"Well," said the young man, "Arthur told me last night; and I took an elder brother's liberty to tell him he had played Leonard a vile trick."

"Godfrey!"

"That would make a much happier nature than Arthur's unhappy, wouldn't it?"

Ruth was too much pained to reply, but she turned and called cheerily, "Father, do you know where Leonard is?"

The father gathered his voice and answered huskily, laying one hand upon his chest, and with the other gesturing up by the Winslow elm to the grove behind it.

She nodded. "Yes!... With Arthur, you say?... Yes!... Thank you!... Yes!" She passed with Godfrey through the wide gate.

"That's like Leonard," said the lover. "He'll tell Arthur he hasn't done a thing he hadn't a perfect right to do."

"And Arthur has not, Godfrey. He has only been less chivalrous than we should have liked him to be. If he had been first in the field, and Leonard had come in and carried her off, you would have counted it a perfect mercy all round."

"Ho-oh! it would have been! Leonard would have made her happy. Arthur never can, and she can never make him so. But what he has done is not all: look how he did it! Leonard was his beloved and best friend"—

"Except his brother Godfrey"—

"Except no one, Ruth, unless it's you. I'm neither persuasive nor kind, nor often with him. Proud of him I was, and never prouder than when I knew him to be furiously in love with her, while yet, for pure, sweet friendship's sake, he kept standing off, standing off."

"I wish you might have seen it, Godfrey. It was so beautiful—and so pitiful!"

"It was manly,—gentlemanly; and that was enough. Then all at once he's taken aback! All control of himself gone, all self-suppression, all conscience"—

"The conscience has returned," said the girl.

"Oh, not to guide him! Only to goad him! Fifty consciences can't honorably undo the mischief now!"

"Did I not write you that there was already, then, a coolness between her and Leonard?"

"Yes; but the whole bigness and littleness of Arthur's small, bad deed lies in the fact that, though he knew that coolness was but a momentary tiff, with Isabel in the wrong, he took advantage of it to push his suit in between and spoil as sweet a match as two hearts were ever making."

"It was more than a tiff, Godfrey; it"—

"Not a bit more! not—a—bit!"

"Yes!—yes—it was a problem! a problem how to harmonize two fine natures keyed utterly unlike. Leonard saw that. That is why he moved so slowly."

"Hmm!" The lover stared away grimly. "I know something about slowness. I suppose it's a virtue—sometimes."

"I think so," said the girl, caressing a flower.

"Ah, well!" responded the other. "She has chosen a nature now that—Oh me!... Ruth, I shall speak to her mother! I am the only one who can. I'll see Mrs. Morris some time this evening, and lay the whole thing out to her as we four see it who have known one another almost from the one cradle."

Ruth smiled sadly. "You will fail. I think the matter will have to go on as it is going. And if it does, you must remember, Godfrey, we do not really know but they may work out the happiest union. At any rate, we must help them to try."

"If they insist on trying, yes; and that will be the best for Leonard."

"The very best. One thing we do know, Godfrey: Arthur will always be a passionate lover, and dear Isabel is as honest and loyal as the day is long."

"The day is not long; this one is not—to me. It's most lamentably short, and to-morrow I must be gone again. I have something to say to you, Ruth, that"—

The maiden gave him a look of sweet protest, which suddenly grew remote as she murmured, "Isabel and her mother are coming out of their front door."

II

ISABEL

There were two dwellings in the Winslow garden,—one as far across at the right of the Byington house as the other was at the left. The one on the right may have contained six or eight bedchambers; the other had but three. The larger stood withdrawn from the public way, a well-preserved and very attractive example of colonial architecture, refined to the point of delicacy in the grace and harmony of its details. Here dwelt Arthur Winslow, barely six weeks a clergyman, alone but for two or three domestics and the rare visits of Godfrey, his only living relation. The other and older house, in the garden's southern front corner, was a gray gambrel-roofed cottage, with its threshold at the edge of the sidewalk; and it was from this cottage that Isabel and her mother stepped, gratefully answering the affectionate wave of Ruth's hand,—Mrs. Morris with the dignity of her forty-odd years, and Isabel with a sudden eager fondness. The next moment the two couples were hidden from each other by the umbrageous garden and by the tall white fence, in which was repeated the architectural grace of the larger house.

Mother and daughter conversed quietly, but very busily, as they came along this enclosure; but presently they dropped their subject to bow cordially across to the father of Ruth, and when he endeavored to say something to them Mrs. Morris moved toward him. Isabel took a step or two more in the direction of the Winslow elm and its inviting bench, but then she also turned. She was of a moderate feminine stature and perfect outline, her step elastic, her mien self-contained, and her face so young that a certain mature tone in her mellow voice was often the cause of Ruth's fond laughter. As winsome, too, she was, as she was beautiful, and "as pink as a rose," said the old-time soldier to himself, as he came down his short front walk, throwing half his glances forward to her, quite unaware that he was equally the object of her admiration.

Though white-haired and somewhat bent he was still slender and handsome, a most worthy figure against the background of the red brick house, whose weathered walls contrasted happily with the blossoming shrubs about their base, and with the green of lawn and trees.

"Good-afternoon, Isabel. I was saying to your mother, I hope such days as this are some offset for the Southern weather and scenery you have had to give up."

"You shouldn't tempt our Southern boastfulness, General," Isabel replied, with an air of meek chiding. She had a pretty way of skirmishing with men which always brought an apologetic laugh from her mother, but which the General had discovered she never used in a company of less than three.

"Oh! ho, ho!" laughed Mrs. Morris, who was just short, plump, and pretty enough to laugh to advantage. "Why, General,"—she sobered abruptly, and she was just pretty and plump and short enough to do this well, also,—"my recovered health is offset enough for me."

"For us, my dear," said the daughter. "My mother's restored health is offset enough for us, General. Indeed, for me"—addressing the distant view—"there is no call for off-set; any landscape or climate is perfect that has such friends in it as—as this one has."

"Oh! ho, ho!" laughed the mother again. Nobody ever told the Morrises they had a delicious Southern accent, and their words are given here exactly as they thought they spoke them.

"My dear," persisted Isabel, rebukingly, "I mean such friends as Ruth Byington."

Mrs. Morris let go her little Southern laugh once more. "Don't you believe her, General—don't you believe her. She means you every bit as much as she means Ruth. She means everybody on Bylow Hill."

"I'm at the mercy of my interpreter," said Isabel. "But I thought"—her eyes went out upon the skyline again—"I thought that men—that men—I thought that men—My dear, you've made me forget what I thought!"

They laughed, all three. Isabel, with a playful sigh, clutched her mother's hand, and the pair drew off and moved away to the bench.

"He puts you in good spirits," said the mother, breaking a silence.

"Good spirits! He puts me in pure heartache. Oh, why did you tell him?"

"Tell him? My child! I have not told him!"

"Oh, mother, do you not see you've told him point-blank that it's all settled?"

"No, dearie, no! I only see that your distress is making you fanciful. But why should he not be told, Isabel?"

"I'm not ready! Oh, I'm not ready! It may suit him well enough to hear it, for he knows Leonard is too fine and great for me; but I'm not ready to tell him."

"My darling, he knows you are good enough for any Leonard he can bring."

"Oh yes, on the plane of the Ten Commandments." The girl smiled unhappily.

"But precious, he loves Arthur deeply, and thinks the world of him."

"Mother, what is it like, to love deeply?"

The query was ignored. "And the old gentleman is fond of you, sweetheart."

"Oh, he likes me. What a tame old invalid that word 'fond' has grown to be! You can be fond of two or three persons at once, nowadays. My soul! I wish I were fond of Arthur Winslow in the old mad way the word meant when it was young!"

"Pshaw, dearie! you'll be fond enough of him, once you're his. He's brilliant, upright, loving and lovable. You see, and say, he is so, and I know your fondness will grow with every day and every experience, happy or bitter."

"Yes.... Yes, I could not endure not to give my love bountifully wherever it rightly belongs. But oh, I wish I had it ready to-day,—a fondness to match his!"

"Now, Isabel! Why, pet, thousands of happy and loving wives will tell you"—

"Oh, I know what they will tell me."

"They'll not tell you they get along without love, dearie. But ten years from now, my daughter, not how fond you were when you first joined hands, but what you have"—

"Oh yes,—been to each other, done for each other, borne from each other, will be the true measure. Oh, of course it will; but there's so much in the right start!"

"Beyond doubt! Understand me, precious: if you have the least ground to fear"—

"Mother! mother! No! no! What! afraid I may love some one else? Never! never! Oh, without boasting, and knowing what I am as well as Leonard Byington knows"—

"Oh, pshaw! Leonard Byington!"

"He knows me, mother,—as if he lived at a higher window that looked down into my back yard." The speaker smiled.

"Then he knows," exclaimed the mother, "you're true gold!"

64

"Yes, but a light coin."

"My pet! He knows you're the tenderest, gentlest dear he ever saw."

"But neither brave nor strong."

"Oh, you not brave! you not strong! You're the lovingest, truest"—

"Only inclined to be a bit too hungry after sympathy, dear."

"You never bid for it, love, never."

"Well, no matter; I shall never love any one but myself too much. I think I shall some day love Arthur as I wish I could love him now. I never did really love Leonard,—I couldn't; I haven't the stature. That was my trouble, dearie: I hadn't the stature. I never shall have; and if it's he you are thinking of, you are wasting your dear, sweet care. But he's going to be our best and nearest friend, mother,—he and Ruth and Godfrey, together and alike. We've so agreed, Arthur and I. Oh, I'm not going to come in here and turn the sweet old nickname of this happy spot into a sneer."

"Then why are you not happy, precious?"

"Happy? Why, my dear, I am happy!"

"With touches of heartache?"

"Oh, with big wrenches of heartache! Why not? Were you never so?"

"I'm so right now, dearie. For after all is said"—

"And thought that can't be said"—murmured Isabel.

"Yes," replied the mother, "after all is said and thought, I should rather give you to Arthur than to any other man I know. Leonard will have a shining career, but it will be in politics."

"I tried to dissuade him," broke in the daughter, "till I was ashamed."

"In politics," continued Mrs. Morris,—"and Northern politics, Isabel. Arthur's will be in the church!"

"Yes," said the other, but her whole attention was within the fence at their side, where a rough stile, made in boyhood days by the two brothers and Leonard, led over into the garden. She sprang up. "Let's go, mother; he's coming!"

"Who, my child?"

"Both! Come, dear, come quickly! Oh, I don't know why we ever came out at all!"

"My dear, it was you proposed it, lest some one should come in!"

The daughter had moved some steps down the road, but now turned again; for Ruth and Godfrey, returning, came out through the garden's high gateway. However, they were giving all their smiles to the greetings which the General sent them from his piazza.

"Come over, mother!" called Isabel, in a stifled voice. "Cross to the hill path!" But before they could reach it Arthur and Leonard came into full view on the stile. Isabel motioned her mother despairingly toward them, wheeled once more, and with a gay call for Ruth's notice hurried to meet her in the middle of the way.

III

ARTHUR AND LEONARD

Godfrey passed over to the General, who had walked down to his gate on his way to the great elm. Out from behind the elm came the other two men, Arthur leading and talking briskly:—

"The sooner the better, Leonard. Now while my work is new and taking shape—Ah! here's Mrs. Morris."

Both men were handsome. Arthur, not much older than Ruth, was of medium height, slender, restless, dark, and eager of glance and speech. Leonard was nearer the age of Godfrey; fairer than Arthur, of a quieter eye, tall, broad-shouldered, powerful, lithe, and almost tamely placid. Mrs. Morris met them with animation.

"Have our churchwarden and our rector been having another of their long talks?"

The joint reply was cut short by Godfrey's imperative hail: "Leonard!"

As Byington turned that way, Arthur said quietly to Mrs. Morris, "He's promised to retain charge"—and nodded toward Isabel. The nod meant Isabel's financial investments.

"And mine?" murmured the well-pleased lady.

"Both."

The two gave heed again to Godfrey, who was loudly asking Leonard, "Why didn't you tell us the news?"

"Oh," drawled Leonard smilingly, "I knew father would."

"I haven't talked with Godfrey since he came," said Mrs. Morris; and as she left Arthur she asked his brother: "What news? Has the governor truly made him"—

"District attorney, yes," said Godfrey. "Ruth, I think you might have told me."

"Godfrey, I think you might have asked me," laughed the girl, drawing Isabel toward Arthur and Leonard, in order to leave Mrs. Morris to Godfrey.

Arthur moved to meet them, but Ruth engaged him with a

67

question, and Isabel turned to Leonard, offering her felicitations with a sweetness that gave Arthur tearing pangs to overhear.

"But when people speak to us of your high office," he could hear her saying, "we will speak to them of your high fitness for it. And still, Leonard, you must let us offer you our congratulations, for it is a high office."

"Thank you," replied Leonard: "let me save the congratulations for the day I lay the office down. Do you, then, really think it high and honorable?"

"Ah," she rejoined, in a tone of reproach and defense that tortured Arthur, "you know I honor the pursuit of the law."

Leonard showed a glimmer of drollery. "Pursuit of the law, yes," he said; "but the pursuit of the lawbreaker"—

"Even that," replied Isabel, "has its frowning honors."

"But I'm much afraid it seems to you," he said, "a sort of blindman's buff played with a club. It often looks so to the pursued, they say."

Isabel gave her chin a little lift, and raised her tone for those behind her: "We shall try not to be among the pursued, Ruth and Arthur and I."

The young lawyer's smile broadened. "My mind is relieved," he said.

"Relieved!" exclaimed Isabel, with a rosy toss. "Ruth, dear, here is your brother in distress lest Arthur or we should embarrass him in his new office by breaking the laws! Mr. Byington, you should not confess such anxieties, even if you are justified in them!"

His response came with meditative slowness and with playful eyes: "Whenever I am justified in having such anxieties, they shall go unconfessed."

"That relieves my fears," laughed Isabel, and caught a quick hint of trouble on Arthur's brow, though he too managed to laugh. Whereupon, half sighing, half singing, she twined an arm in one of Ruth's, swung round her, waved to the General as he took a seat on the elm-tree bench, and so, passing to Arthur, changed partners.

"Let us go in," whispered Leonard to his sister, with a sudden pained look, and instantly resumed his genial air.

But the uneasy Arthur saw his moving lips and both changes of countenance. He saw also the look which Ruth threw toward Mrs. Morris, where that lady and Godfrey moved slowly in conversation,—he ever so sedate, she ever so sprightly. And he saw Isabel glance as anxiously in the same direction. But then her eyes came to his, and under her voice, though with a brow all sunshine, she said, "Don't look so perplexed."

"Perplexed!" he gasped. "Isabel, you're giving me anguish!"

She gleamed an injured amazement, but promptly threw it off, and when she turned to see if Leonard or Ruth had observed it they were moving to meet Godfrey. Mrs. Morris was joining the General under the elm.

"How have I given you pain, dear heart?" asked Isabel, as she and Arthur took two or three slow steps apart from the rest, so turning her face that they should see its tender kindness.

"Ah! don't ask me, my beloved!" he warily exclaimed. "It is all gone! Oh, the heavenly wonder to hear you, Isabel Morris, you—give me loving names! You might have answered me so differently; but your voice, your eyes, work miracles of healing, and I am whole again."

Isabel gave again the laugh whose blithe, final sigh was always its most winning note. Then, with tremendous gravity, she said, "You are very indiscreet, dear, to let me know my power."

His face clouded an instant, as if the thought startled him with its truth and value. But when she added, with yet deeper seriousness of brow, "That's no way to tame a shrew, my love," he laughed aloud, and peace came again with Isabel's smile.

Then—because a woman must always insist on seeing the wrong side of the goods—she murmured, "Tell me, Arthur, what disturbed you."

"Words, Isabel, mere words of yours, which I see now were meant in purest play. You told Leonard"—

"Leonard! What did I tell Leonard, dear?"

"You told him not to confess certain anxieties, even if they were justified."

"Oh, Arthur!"

"I see my folly, dearest. But Isabel, he ought not to have answered that the more they were justified, the more they should go unconfessed!"

"Oh, Arthur! the merest, idlest prattle! What meaning could you"—

"None, Isabel, none! Only, my good angel, I so ill deserve you that with every breath I draw I have a desperate fright of losing you, and a hideous resentment against whoever could so much as think to rob me of you."

"Why, dear heart, don't you know that couldn't be done?"

"Oh, I know it, you being what you are, even though I am only what I am. But, Isabel, you know he loves you. No human soul is strong enough to blow out the flame of the love you kindle, Isabel

69

Morris, as one would blow out his bedroom candle and go to sleep at the stroke of a clock."

"Arthur, I believe Leonard—and I do not say it in his praise—I believe Leonard can do that!"

"No, not so, not so! Leonard is strong, but the fire of a strong man's love, however smothered, burns on without mercy, my beautiful, and you cannot go in and out of that burning house as though it were not on fire."

"And shall Leonard, then, not be our nearest and best friend, as we had planned?"

"He shall, Isabel. Ah yes; not one smallest part of your sweet friendship will I take from him, nor of his from you. For, Isabel, though he were as weak as I"—

"As weak as I, you should say, dear. You are not weak, Arthur, are you?"

"Weak as the bending grass, Isabel, under this load of love. But though he, I say, were as weak as I, you—ah, you!—are as wise as you are bewitching; and if I should speak to you from my most craven fear, I could find but one word of warning."

"Oh, you dear, blind flatterer! And what word would that be?"

"That you are most bewitching when you are wisest."

As Isabel softly laughed she cast a dreaming glance behind, and noticed that she and Arthur were quite hidden in the flowery undergrowth of the hill path. They kissed.

"Beloved," said her worshipper, with a clouded smile, as he let her down from her tiptoes, "do you know you took that as though you were thinking of something else?"

"Did I? Oh, I didn't mean to."

Such a reply only darkened the cloud. "Of whom were you thinking, Isabel?"

She blushed. "I was think—thinking—why, I was—I—I was think—thinking"—she went redder and redder as he went pale—"thinking of everybody on Bylow Hill. Why—why, dear heart, don't you see? When you"—

"Oh, enough, enough, my angel! I take the question back!"

"You made me think of everybody, Arthur, you were so sudden. Just suppose I had done so to you!" They both thought that worthy of a good laugh. "Next time, dear," added Isabel,—"no, no, no, but—next time, you mustn't be so sudden. There's no need, you know,"—she blushed again,—"and I promise you I'll give my whole mind to it! Get me some of that hawthorn bloom yonder, and let's go back."

70

IV

AND BRING DOWN THE REMAINDER

This "hill path" was a narrowed continuance of the street, that led gradually down along the hill's steep face to reach the town and the river meadows. Godfrey, halting before Ruth and her brother, watched the blooming hawthorn, over there, bend and shake and straighten and bend again, above Arthur's unseen hands. Then, glancing furtively back toward Mrs. Morris, he muttered to Ruth, while Leonard gravely looked out across the landscape, "I live and learn."

"So we learn to live," was Ruth's playful reply. To her it was painfully clear that Mrs. Morris, very sweetly no doubt, had eluded Godfrey's endeavors to inform her of anything not to his brother's unqualified praise. In the Bylow Hill group, Ruth had a way of smiling abstractedly, which was very dear to Godfrey even when it meant he had best say no more; and this smile had just said this to him when Isabel and Arthur came into view again. As the two and the three drifted toward each other, Ruth let Leonard outstep her, and joined Godfrey with a light in her face that quickened his pulse.

After a word or two of slight import she said, as they slowly walked, "Godfrey."

"Yes," eagerly responded the lover.

"Down in the garden, awhile ago—did I—promise something?"

"You most certainly did!" She had promised that if he would let a certain subject drop she would bring it up again, herself, before he must take his leave.

"And must you go very soon, now?" she asked.

"I've only a few minutes left," said the lover, with a lover's license.

"Well, I'm ready to speak. Of course, Godfrey, I know my heart."

The young man smiled ruefully. "I've known mine till I'm dead tired of the acquaintance."

Other words passed, her eyes on the ground as they loitered,

71

and after a pause she murmured:—"But I've known my heart as long as you've known yours."

"You've known—What do you—Oh, Ruth, look at me!"

She looked, very tenderly, although she said, "You forget we are observed."

"Oh, observed! Do you mean hope—for me—after all?"

"I mean that if you will only wait until we can get a clear light on this matter of Isabel's—which will most likely be by the next time you come"—

"Oh, Ruth, Ruth, my own Ruth at last!"

"Please don't speak so. I'm not engaging myself to you now."

"Oh yes, you are! Yes, you are! Yes—you—are!"

"No—no—no—listen! Listen to me, Godfrey. I think that now, among us all, we shall manage Isabel's affair well enough, and that the very next time—you—come"—She began absently to pick her steps.

"What—what then?"

"Then you may ask me."

The response of the overjoyed lover was but one or two passionate words, and her sufficient reply, as they halted among their fellows, was to look across the valley with her meditative smile. Isabel took note, but kindly gave a long sigh of admiration, and with an exalted sweep of the hand drew the gaze of the five to the beauties of the scene below. The day was near its end. The long shadow of the great cliff behind Bylow Hill hung over the roofs of the town and over the hither meadows. The sun's rays were laying their last touches upon the winding river, and upon the grainfields that extended from its farther shore. In the upper blue rested a few peaceful clouds, changing from silver to pink, from pink to pearly gray, and on the skyline crouched in a purpling haze the round-backed mountains of another county.

To Mrs. Morris and the General the sight, from the old elm-tree seat, was even fairer than to the youthful group whose forms stood out against the sky, the floral colors of the girls' draperies heightened by the western light. For a while the two sitters gave the perfect scene the tribute of a perfect silence, and then the General asked, as he cautiously straightened his impaired frame, "Has not Isabel been making some—eh—news for herself—and us?"

The lady's lips parted for their peculiar laugh of embarrassment, but the questioner's smile was so serious that she forced her sweetest gravity. "Why, General, according to our Southern ways," she said,—every word mellowed by her Southern way of saying it,—"that's for Isabel to tell you."

72

"Then why does she not do it, Mrs. Morris?" asked the veteran, who had been district attorney himself once upon a time, and was clever with witnesses.

"Why, really, General, Isabel hasn't had a cha—Oh! ho, ho! I oughtn't to have said that!" Mrs. Morris had a killing dimple, but never used it.

"I suppose—of course"—said the General, "she will say it's—eh—Arthur?"

"Now you're making me tell," she laughed, "and I mustn't! General, Godfrey seems to be going."

In fact, Godfrey was shaking hands with Ruth and Leonard. Now he took the hands of Arthur and Isabel together, and Mrs. Morris laughed more sweetly and with more oh's and ho's than ever; for Isabel sedately kissed Arthur's brother.

Ruth made signs to her father, who answered them in kind. "What does she say, Mrs. Morris? Can you hear?"

"She says they're singing 'your hymn' down in a church under the hill."

"Ah yes." He beamed and nodded to Ruth; but when Mrs. Morris once more laughed, his brow clouded a trifle. "Your daughter, Mrs. Morris"—

The lady broke in with a note of bright surprise, rose, and took an unconscious step forward. The five young friends were advancing in a compact cluster, with measured pace. Ruth and Isabel, in front abreast, and making happy show of the hawthorn sprays, were just enough apart to conceal, except for their superior height, the three lovers, and in lowered tones, but with kindling eyes, the five, incited by Ruth, were singing the song they had caught up from the valley,—the old man's favorite from the days of his own song-time. The General got himself hurriedly to his feet; the shade passed from his brow. The group came close; he stepped out, and Isabel, meeting him, laid her two hands in his, while the halting cluster ceased their song suspensively on a line that pledged loves and friendships too ethereal to clash.

"Isabel,"—he turned up a broadened palm,—"here's my amen to that line; where's yours?"

With blushing alacrity she laid her hand on his.

"Arthur!" he called, and the lively lover added his to the two. "Now, Ruth!"

"Father!" laughed the daughter, "isn't this rather youngish?" But she laid her hand promptly upon Arthur's, and the lines of the General's face deepened playfully, and Mrs. Morris's dimple did the same, as Godfrey thrust his hand in upon Ruth's, unasked. The matron laughed very tenderly on the key of O while she added her hand, and received Leonard's heavy palm above it. Then Arthur clapped a second hand upon Leonard's, and Leonard was about to lay a second quietly upon Arthur's, when Isabel, rose-red from brow to throat, gayly broke the heap and embraced Ruth.

"Well, honey-girlie," said Mrs. Morris, as she and Isabel reentered their cottage, "wasn't it sweet of them all, that 'laying on of hands,' as Arthur called it?"

"Yes," replied the Southern girl, starting up the cramped old New England stairway to her room. "It was child's play, but it was very sweet of them, and especially of the General."

The mother detained her fondly. "And still, my child, you're not satisfied?"

"Ah, mother, are you blind, stone blind, or do you only hope I am?"

"My dearie!"

"Why, mother, excepting Leonard, we haven't had one word of true consent from one of them."

"Oh, now, Isabel! They'll all be glad enough by and by."

"Yes," said the daughter, from the landing above, "I've no doubt of that."

She passed into her room, closed the door, and standing in the middle of the floor, with her temples in her palms, said, "O merciful God! Oh, Leonard Byington, if only that second hand of yours had hung back!"

V

SKY AND POOL

Arthur and Isabel were married in their own little church of All Angels, at the far end of the old street.

"I cal'late," said a rustic member of his vestry, "th' never was as pretty a weddin' so simple, nor as simple a weddin' so pretty!"

Because he said it to Leonard Byington he ended with a manly laugh, for by the anxious glance of his spectacled daughter he knew he had slipped somewhere in his English. But when he heard Leonard and Ruth, in greeting the bride's mother, jointly repeat the sentiment as their own, he was, for a moment, nearly as happy as Mrs. Morris.

"Such a pity Godfrey had to be away!" said Mrs. Morris. It was the only pity she chose to emphasize.

Godfrey was on distant seas. The north-bound mid-afternoon express bore away the bridal pair for a week's absence.

"Too short," said a friend or so whom Leonard fell in with as he came from the railway station, and Leonard admitted that Arthur was badly in need of rest.

At sunset Ruth came out of her gate and stood to welcome her brother's tardy return. Both brightly smiled; neither spoke.

When he gave her a letter with a foreign stamp her face lighted gratefully, but still without words she put it under her belt. Then they joined hands, and he asked, "Where's father?"

"Inside on the lounge," she replied. Her lips fell into their faraway smile, to which she added this time a murmur as of reverie, and Leonard said almost as musingly, "Come, take a short turn."

They moved on to the Winslow gate, and entered the garden by a path which brought them to a point midway between the old cottage and the larger house. There it crossed under an arch transecting an arbor that extended from a side door of the one dwelling to a like one of the other, and the brother and sister had just passed this embowered spot and were stepping down a winding descent by which the path sought the old mill-pond, when behind them they observed two women pass athwart their track by way of the arbor, and Ruth smiled and murmured again. The crossing pair were Mrs. Morris and Sarah Stebbens, the Winslows' life-long housekeeper, deeply immersed in arranging for Isabel to become lady of the larger house, while her mother, with a single young maidservant, was to remain mistress of the cottage.

The deep pond to whose edge Leonard and Ruth presently came was a narrow piece of clear water held in between Bylow Hill and the loftier cliff beyond by an old stone dam long unused. Rude ledges of sombre rock underlay its depths and lined and shelved its sides. Broad beeches and dark hemlocks overhung it. At every turn it mirrored back the slanting forms of the white and the yellow birch, or slept under green mantles of lily pads. It bore a haunted air even in the floweriest days of the year, when every bird of the wood thrilled it with his songs, and it gave to the entire region the gravest as well as richest note among all its harmonies. Down the whole way to it some one long gone had gardened with so wise a hand that later negligence had only made the wild loveliness of this inmost refuge more affluent and impassioned.

At one point, where the hemlocks hung farthest and lowest over the pool, and the foot sank deep in a velvet of green mosses, a solid ledge of dark rock shelved inward from the top of the bank and down through the flood to a depth cavernous and black. Here, brought from time to time by the Byington and Winslow playmates, lay a number of mossy stones rounded by primeval floods, some large enough for seats, some small; and here, where Ruth had last sat with Godfrey, she now came with her brother.

The habitual fewness of Leonard's words was a thing she prized beyond count. It made Mrs. Morris nervous, drained her mind's treasury, and sent her conversational powers borrowing and begging; Isabel it awed; Arthur it tantalized; to Godfrey it was an appetizing drollery; but to Ruth it was dearer and clearer than all spoken eloquence.

The same trait in her, only less marked, was as satisfying to him, and from one rare utterance to another their thoughts moved like consorted ships from light to light along a home coast. A motion, a glance, a gleam, a shade, told its tale, as across leagues of silence a shred of smoke may tell one dweller in the wilderness the way or want of another. Such converse may have been a mere phase of the New Englander's passion for economy, or only the survival of a primitive spiritual commerce which most of us have lost through the easier use of speech and print; but the sister took calm delight in it, and it bound the two to each other as though it were itself a sort of goodness or greatness.

"They have it of their mother," the old General sometimes said to himself.

There were moments, too, when their intercourse was still more subtle, and now they sat without exchange of glance or gesture, silent as chess players, looking up the narrow water into a sunset exquisite in the delicacy of its silvery plumes, fleeces pink and dusk, and illimitable distances of palest green seen through fan-rays of white light shot down from one dark, unthreatening cloud.

"Leonard," at length said the sister, as if she had studied every possibility on the board before touching the chosen piece, "couldn't you go away for a time?"

And with deliberate readiness the other gentle voice replied, "I don't think I'd better."

While they spoke their gaze rested on the changing beauties of pool and sky, and after the brief inquiry and response it still remained, though the inner glow of their mutual love and worship deepened and warmed as did the colors of the heavens and of the glassing waters. The brother knew full well Ruth's poignant sense of his distresses; and to her his mute tongue and unbent head were a sister's convincement that he would endure them in a manner wholly faithful to every one of the loved hands that had lain under his the evening Godfrey had said good-by.

Indeed, it was clear that to go away—unless he honestly felt too weak to remain—would be unfair to almost every person, every interest, concerned; and such a step was but second choice in Ruth's mind, conditioned solely on any unreadiness he might have uprightly to bear the burden brought upon him by—well, after all, by his own too confident miscalculations in the game of hearts.

To him such flight signified the indeterminate continuance of his sister's maiden singleness and a like prolongation of her lover's galling suspense. To Ruth it stood not only for the loss of her brother, but for the narrowing of their father's already narrowed life,—a narrowing which might come to mean a shortening as well; and it meant also the leaving of Isabel and Arthur to their mistake and to their unskilfulness slowly and patiently to work out its cure. To go away were, for him, to consent to be the one unbroken string on a noble but difficult instrument. These thoughts and many more like them passed to and fro, out through the abstracted eyes of the one, across to the fading clouds, and back through the abstracted eyes and into the responding heart of the other.

At length the sister rose. "I must go to father," she said.

The brother stood up. Their eyes exchanged a gentle gaze and tenderly contracted.

"I will come presently," he replied, and was turning toward the water, when he paused, threw a hand toward the steep wood across the pool, and silently bade her listen.

The note he had remotely heard was rare on Bylow Hill since the town had come in below, and one of the errands which oftenest brought the hill's dwellers to this nook in solitary pairs was to hearken for that voice of unearthly rapture,—a rapture above all melancholy and beyond all mirth,—the call of the hermit thrush.

Now the waiting seemed in vain. The brother's hand sank, the sister turned, and soon he saw her pass from view among the boughs as she wound up the rambling path toward the three homes.

At the top she halted, still longing to hear at his side that marvellous wood-note, and was just starting on once more, when from the same quarter as before it came again, with new and fervent clearness. With noiseless foot she sprang back down the bendings of the path, having no other thought but to find her brother standing as she had left him, a rapt hearer of the heavenly strain.

She reached the spot, but found no hearkening or standing form. The young man's stalwart frame lay prone on the green bank, where he had thrown himself the moment she had left his sight, and his face was buried in the deep moss.

The stir of her swift coming reached his ear barely in time for him, as she choked down a cry that had all but escaped her, to turn upon his back, meet her glance, and drive the agony from his face with a languorous smile. The melting song pervaded the air, but neither of them lifted a noting finger.

Leonard rose to his feet. Ruth gave him a hand and then its fellow, and as he pressed them together she said, "I wish you would go away for a time."

He dropped one of her hands, and keeping the other, started slowly homeward; and it was not until they had climbed half the ascent that, with his most remote yet boyish smile, he replied, "I don't think I'd better."

VI

IN THE PUBLIC EYE

August, September, October, November,—so passed the year in gorgeous recession over Bylow Hill. Among their dismantled trees the three homes stood unveiled to the town on the meadows and to travellers who looked from train windows while crossing the river bridge. To those who inquired whose they were there was always some one more than ready to give names and details, and to tell how perfect a bond ever had been—how beautiful a fellowship was yet, now—up there.

Sevenfold they called it, although one of the seven was away; namely, Lieutenant Godfrey Winslow, of the navy, famed for his splendid behavior in the late so-and-so affair. That stately house at the right, they said, was his home what brief times the sea was not.

There lived, it would be added, his younger brother, so rapidly coming into note,—the eccentric but gifted rector of All Angels; whose great success in the heart of a Congregational community was due hardly more to his high talents than to the combined winsomeness and practical sympathies of his beautiful bride, or to the resourceful wisdom and zeal of his churchwarden, Leonard Byington.

"Any relation to Byington, your new political leader in these parts?"

"Same man," the answer would be, and there the narrator was sure to fall into a glowing tribute to the ideal companionship existing between the rector, his bride, the young district attorney, and Ruth Byington.

What made this intimacy the more interesting was, in the eyes of a growing number of observers, that, as they said, "Arthur Winslow was not always an affable man, and was much more rarely a happy one."

Behind and above this popular verdict was that of the old street behind and above the town,—a sort of revised version, a higher criticism. If the young rector, this old street explained, oftener looked anxious than complacent, so in their time, most likely, did St. Paul and St. Peter. If he was not always affable, why, neither are volcanoes; the man was all molten metal within. Anyhow, he filled his church to the doors.

Coaching parties of the vastly rich made the town their Sunday stopping place purely to hear him; not so much because the boldness of his speculations kept his bishop frightened as because he always fused those speculations on, white-hot, to the daily issues of private and public life, in a way to make pampered ladies hold their breath, and men of the world their brows. Such a man, to whom the least sin seemed black and bottomless, yet who appeared to know by experience the soul's every throe in the foulest crimes, was not going to show his joys on the surface in quips and smiles.

"You should have heard," said the old street, "his sermon to husbands and wives! His own bride turned pale. He turned pale himself."

It was wonder enough that even the bride could be happy, at such an altitude, so to speak; immersing herself utterly, as she did, in the interests that devoured him. All Angels forgot his gloom in the radiance of her charms,—the sweet genuineness of her formal pieties, the tender glow and universality of her sympathies, the witchery of her ever ready, never too ready playfulness. It was captivating to see how instantly and entirely she had fitted herself into a partnership so exacting; though it was pitiful to note, on second glance, how the tint and contour of her cheek were losing their perfection, and her eyes were showing those rapid alternations of languor and vivacity which story-tellers call a "hunted look." Yet, oh, yes, she was happy; the pair were happy. It was as a pair that they were happiest. Else, said the old street, they could not keep up the old Winslow-Byington alliance so beautifully.

To the truth of this general outline the three homes' domestics, dominated by Sarah Stebbens, certified with cordial and loyal brevity. Yet when Ruth wrote Godfrey how well things were going, there lurked between her bright lines one or two irrepressible meanings that locked his jaws till they creaked.

In fact, both his brother and hers were "ailing." Both carried a jaded, almost a broken look, and Arthur was taking things to make him eat and sleep; while Leonard had daily accepted more and more of the young rector's complicating cares, until he was really the parish's chief burden-bearer.

"No," he said to his father, "Arthur carries his whole work manfully on his own shoulders."

"But, my son," replied the old General, "don't you see you're carrying Arthur?"

"No, I sha'n't do that," dryly responded the son; but Ruth saw a change on his brow as on that of a guide who fears he has missed the path.

The four young friends spent many delightful evenings together in the Winslow house, with Mrs. Morris and the General on one side at cribbage. Ruth had frequent happy laughs, observing Isabel's gift for making Leonard talk. It gave her a new joy in both of them to have the lovely hostess draw him out, out, out, on every matter in the wide arena to which he so vitally belonged; eliciting a flow of speech so animated that only afterward did one notice how dumb as any tree on Bylow Hill he had been in regard to himself.

"They are bow and violin," said Arthur to Ruth, with his dark, unsmiling face so free from resentment that she gratefully wondered at him, and was presently ashamed to find herself asking her own mind if he was growing too subtle for her.

On these occasions Isabel was wont to court Ruth's counsel concerning her wifely part in Arthur's work, thus often getting Leonard's as well. Sometimes she impeached his masculine view of things, in her old skirmishing way. Then she would turn rose-color once more and mirthfully sigh, while Ruth laughed and wished for Godfrey, and Mrs. Morris breathed soft ho-ho's from the cribbage board.

So came the Thanksgiving season, with strong, black ice on the mill pond, where the four skated hand in hand. Then the piling snows stopped the skating with a white Christmas, the old year sank to rest, the new rose up, and Bylow Hill, under its bare elms and with the pine-crested ridge at its back, sat in the cold sunshine like a white sea bird with its head in its down. And when the nights were frigid and clear its ruddy lights of lamp and hearth seemed to answer the downward gaze of the stars in silent gratitude for conditions of happiness strangely perfect for this imperfect world, and the town marvelled at the young rector's grasp of his subject when his text was, "The heart knoweth his own bitterness."

VII

THE HOUR STRIKES

But on a day in the very last of winter, when every one was in the thick of all the year's tasks and cares, there came to Leonard this letter:—

LEONARD BYINGTON, ESQUIRE:

SIR,—I find myself compelled to ask that you consider your acquaintanceship with my wife at an end. Doubtless this request will give you more relief than surprise. The visible waste of your frame and the loss of her exquisite bloom are proof enough that both you and she have long been in daily dread of a far worse visitation. It is not worse, because I know how sentimental your impotent and conscience-plagued interchanges of affection have been. I shall permit and assist you to keep this matter a secret. To let it be known would instantly wreck your own career, and would blast at a breath the fortunes of our church and of every one of both our kindreds. I will therefore not at this time require you to resign your church office or to break off those business intimacies with me which, though no longer founded in personal esteem, are vital to interests that common decency must move you to shield from new peril.

I ask for no repair of the inextinguishable wrong you have done me. I only ask you not to fancy that I am to be beguiled by arguments or denials or moved by threats, or that one word I here write is founded on conjecture or inference. Grovelling at my feet, in sobs of shame and with prayers for pardon, Isabel has told me all. Has told me all, Leonard Byington, my once trusted friend. Now, though prostrated on her bed, she rejoices in the double

82

forgiveness of her husband and her priest, blessing him for deliverance from the misleadings of one who—great God! must I write it?—might at last have dragged her into crime. It is her request, as it is my command, that you darken our threshold no more, and that as far as practicable you keep yourself from her sight.

Faithfully,
ARTHUR WINSLOW

With his swivel-chair overturned behind him the young lawyer stood at the desk of his inner office, read this letter through at headlong speed, turned it again, and re-read it slowly, searchingly, from his own name to its writer's.

Then readjusting his chair he stepped to a door, asked a clerk in the outer office to order his cutter, turned back, and was closing his desk, when his partner came to him.

"Byington, are you ill?" asked the fatherly man.

"No; I'm only going out on some business. I'll be back about—" He looked at his watch.

"Byington, don't go. You're ill. You don't realize how ill you are. If you go at all, go home, and let me send some one with you. Why, your hand is as cold"—

"I'm all right," said the young man, freeing his hand and smiling with white lips. He took his hat and passed out.

Meanwhile Isabel lay on her bed too overwhelmed to rise. In his room adjoining, with doors locked, Arthur paced the floor. He had spent the first half of the night in an agonizing interview with his wife, and the second half in writing and rewriting the letter to Leonard.

Now Isabel noticed the cessation of his steps. In the door between them the key turned; then the door opened, and he stood, haggard and dishevelled, gazing on her. She sat up in the bed, wan, tear-spent, her glorious hair falling over the embroideries of her nightdress.

"Arthur, dear, I am sorry for every angry word I have spoken. But the things I have denied I must deny forever.

"If you should wait till doomsday, I could confess no more.

"I have never harbored one throb of unworthy or unsafe regard toward any man in this wide world.

"For me to say differently would be to lie in God's own face.

"I have had great happiness of Leonard's companionship, and I have been proud to be myself a proof that a man and a woman can be close, dear, daily friends without being lovers or kin, and earth be only more like heaven for it, to them and all theirs. If Leonard has confessed one word more than that for me,—or even for himself, Arthur, dearest,—he has lost his reason. It's a frightful explanation, but I find no other.

"Leonard Byington is not wicked, and if he were he wouldn't be so in a dastard's way.

"Never since the day I first plighted my faith to you, dear heart, has he given me one sign of a lover's love.

"Oh, Arthur, I do love my husband! This night has proved it to me as I never knew it before; and if you will only believe me and go back to Leonard, I believe he can tear the mask off this horrible mystery."

Arthur turned and once more locked the door. His wife flamed red and hearkened, and the light footfall which had tortured her for hours began again. Suddenly she left the bed and hurried to dress.

At the mirror, with her hair lifted on her hands, she paused and again hearkened. Sleighbells stopped at the front door.

Now some one was let in down there, and now, at her husband's room, Giles, his English man of all work, announced Mr. Byington:—

"Yes, sir, but he says if you can't come down 'e will 'ave to come up, sir."

VIII

GIVE YOU FIVE MINUTES

As Arthur entered the library Leonard came from its farther end, and they halted on opposite sides of a large table. Arthur was flushed and looked fearfully spent. Leonard was pale.

"I have your letter, Arthur."

The rector bowed. He gave a start, but tried to conceal a gleam of triumph.

Leonard ignored it and spoke on:—

"A gentleman, Arthur,—I mean any one trying to be a whole gentleman,—is a very helpless creature, nowadays, in matters of this sort."

He looked formidable, and as he lightly grasped a chair at his side it seemed about to be turned into a weapon.

"The old thing once called satisfaction," he continued, "is something one can no longer either ask or offer, in any form. He can neither rail, nor strike, nor spellbind, nor challenge, nor lampoon, nor prosecute."

"Nearly as helpless as a clergyman," said Arthur.

"Almost," replied the visitor. "No, there is no more satisfaction in any of those things, for him, than if he were all a clergyman is supposed to be. There is none even in saying this, to you, here, now, and I'm not here to say it. Neither am I here to vindicate myself—no, nor yet Isabel—with professions or arguments to you; I might as well argue with a forest fire."

"Quite as well. What are you here for?"

"Be patient and I'll tell you; I'm trying to be so with you."

"You—trying"—

"Stop that nonsense, Arthur. Ah me, Arthur Winslow, I have no wish to humiliate you. Through the loyalty of your wife's pure heart, whatever humiliates you must humiliate her. Oh, I could wish her in her shroud and coffin rather than have her suffer the humiliation you have prepared for yourself and for her through you."

Arthur showed a thrill of alarm. "Do you propose to go down to public shame and drag us all with you?"

"No, nor to let you, if I can prevent you. Arthur, you have allowed a base jealousy to persuade you, in the face of every contrary evidence, that your fair young wife has lost her loyalty— and your nearest friend the commonest honesty—in a clandestine love. Under the goadings of that passion you have foully guessed, have heartlessly accused, have brazenly lied. Isabel has confessed nothing to you, and I know by your lies to me how pusillanimously you must have been lying to her. Had your guess been right, I should not have known you were only guessing, and your successful iniquity would have remained hidden from everybody but yourself— I still do you the honor to believe you would have realized it. Now the vital question is, do you realize it, and will you undo it?"

Arthur was deadly pale; his pointing finger trembled. "Leave"—he choked—"leave this house."

Leonard turned scarlet, but his tone sank low. "Arthur, I don't believe your soul is rotten. If I did, I should not be such a knave or such a fool as to make any treaty with you that would leave you in your pulpit one Sabbath Day."

"What do you—what do you mean by that?"

"I mean that such a treaty would be foul faith to everybody."

"So, then, you do propose one common shipwreck for us all."

"Quite the contrary. To trust the fortunes of our loved ones to any treaty with a rotten soul would indeed be to launch them upon a stormy sea in a rotten boat. But I do not believe your soul is so. I believe it is sound,—still sound, though on fire; and so, to help you quench its burning, I give you my pledge to be from this day a stranger to your sweet wife. And now will you do something for me, to prove that your soul is sound and is going to stay sound? It shall be the least I can ask in good faith to the world we live in."

"What is it?" asked Arthur. There was no capitulation in his face or his voice.

"I want you to make to Isabel a full retraction and explanation of every falsehood you have uttered to her or to me in this matter." Leonard was pale again; Arthur burned red a moment, and then turned paler than Leonard.

"You fiend!" gasped the husband. "I am to exalt you, and abase myself, to her?"

"No. No, Arthur. Women are strange; every chance is that in her eyes I shall be abased." The speaker went whiter than ever.

"But be that as it may, you shall have lifted your soul out of the mire. You must do it, Arthur; don't you see you must?"

86

Arthur sank into the chair at his side. He seemed to have guessed what Leonard was keeping unsaid. A moisture of anguish stood on his brow. Yet—

"I will die before I will do it," he said.

Leonard drew forth the letter, and then his watch. "Arthur Winslow, I give you five minutes. If you don't make me that promise in that time, I shall this day show this letter to your bishop."

The rector sat clenching his fingers and spreading them again, and staring at the table.

A bead of sweat, then a second, and then a third started down his forehead.

Presently he clutched the board, drew himself to his feet, and turned to leave the chair, but fell across its arms, slid heavily from them, and with one rude thump and then another lay unconscious on the floor.

Leonard sprang round the table, but when he would have lifted the fallen head it was in the arms of Isabel, and her dilated eyes were on him in a look of passionate aversion.

"Ring!" she cried. "Ring for Sarah—and go!

"No! stop! don't ring! he's coming to! Only go! go quickly and forever! Say not a word,—oh, not a word! I heard it all! Despise me too, for I listened at the door!

"Oh, my husband! Arthur, look at me, Arthur. Look, Arthur; it's your Isabel. Oh, Arthur, my husband, my husband!"

IX

THE YOUNG YEAR SMILES

Martin Kelly, pious Irishman and out-door factotum of the Byington place, paused from the last snow-shovelling of the season to reply to a wandering salesman of fruit trees.

"Mr. Airthur Winslow or Mr. Linnard Boyington,—naw, sor! ye can see nayther the wan nor th' other, whatsomiver! How can ye see thim, moy graciouz! whin 'tis two weeks since the two o' thim was tuck the same noight wid the pneumonias, boy gorra! and the both of thim has thim on the loongs!"

The nursery agent asked how it had happened so.

"Hawh! ask yer grandmother! All ye can say is they was roipe to catch the maladee, whatsomiver! Ye cannot always tell how 'tis catched, and whin ye cannot tell, moy graciouz! ye have got the wurrst koind!"

The two sick men recovered very nearly at the same time.

One day when Leonard had read all his accumulated mail and had seen three or four men officially in his bedchamber, he told Ruth that a certain criminal case, the trial of which had been waiting for his recovery, would take him to the county-seat, and would keep him there many days, probably weeks, except for brief visits to his office and yet briefer moments at home.

Ruth gave him a look of tender approval, laid a hand in his, and bent into the evening fire her far-off smile. Thus, and only thus, he knew she had divined what had befallen.

A day or two afterward Mrs. Morris brought him a note from Arthur. He wrote an answer while she stayed, and while Ruth listened elatedly to her sprightly account of how well Isabel still bore the burden of nursing a most loving but most nervous husband.

The missive from Arthur was a short but complete and propitiative acknowledgment of his error and fraility. It offered no change in the agreement as to Isabel, but it professed a high yet humble resolve to fall no more, and it ended with a manly offer to resign his pulpit, and even to lay aside his sacred calling, if Leonard retained any belief in the moral necessity of his so doing.

Leonard's reply was a very brief exhortation to his friend to put away all thought of resigning, and to take up his work again with the zeal with which he had first entered upon it.

Mrs. Morris went away refreshed, and left the Byingtons equally so. Her buoyancy had been as prettily restrained, her sympathies as sweet, her dimple as unconscious, her belief in everybody's wit and wisdom except her own as genuine, and her timid dissimulations as kindly meant and as transparent, as ever. Yet there was an unspoken compassion for her when she was gone, for in the parting words with which she playfully vaunted her ignorance of the correspondence she was bearing, it was clear, even to the General, that behind that small ignorance she had a larger knowledge,—a fact that made her dainty cheerfulness seem very brave.

The freshets swept down the valleys, the myriad yellow twigs of the brookside willows turned green, a cheery piping rose from the ponds, the last gleam of snow passed from the farthest hills, the bluebird sang, the harrow followed the plough, Ruth's crocuses shone above the greening sod, and down by the old mill-pool and on the steep hillside beyond it she and Isabel gathered arbutus, anemones, and the yellow violet. Spring had come.

Then through the thickening greenery the dogwood shone like belated drifts, the flashing warblers passed on into the north, the bobolink had arrived, the robin was already overeating, the whole chorus of birds that had come to nest and stay broke forth, and it was summer.

Leonard was back in his own town, enriched with new esteem from the public and from the men of his profession. The noted case was won, a victory for the peace and dignity of the state, due wholly, it was said, to the energy and sagacity of the young district attorney. A murder had been so cunningly done that suspicion could fasten nowhere, until Byington laid his finger upon a man of so unspotted a name that no one else had had the mental courage to point to him. Through a long and masterly untangling of contradictions the state's counsel had so overwhelmingly proved him guilty that he had confessed without waiting for the jury's verdict.

"Yes," said many, "it was a great stroke, Leonard's management of that thing." And not a few added that it had made him an older man—"that or something." Those who were of his politics, and even some who were not, stopped him in Main Street and State Street to "shake" and to say, without too much care for logical sequence, how soon, in their opinion, he would be the commonwealth's "favorite son."

"My dear Mrs. Morris," said the General, "every town has at least one." But even Mrs. Morris could see the father's faith and pride through the old soldier's satire.

X

THE STORM REGATHERS

On the other hand, things were going ill with the little church of All Angels. Arthur kept his people as tensely strung as ever, but he no longer drew from them the chords of aspiration and enterprise. It was a sad disenchantment, and none the less so because no one seemed to know what the matter was. One darkly guessed he was writing a book, and the vestryman who had praised the lovely simplicity of the wedding lucidly explained that the young rector had "lost his grip."

At times there were flashes of recovery. One Sabbath the whole congregation came out under his benediction uplifted by his word that "loving is living."

"The more we love," they quoted him on their various ways home, "the more we live. The deeper we love, the deeper we live. The more selfishly or unselfishly, the higher, the broader, the purer, the wiser, we love, the more selfishly or unselfishly, the higher, the broader, the purer, the wiser, we live!" The rector's gentle wife was visibly and ever so prettily rejoiced.

True, but hardly the whole truth. In her mother's cottage her smiles were almost sad, and when she had crossed the garden and got into her own room she dropped upon her bed and wept. Yet she quickly ceased, and put on again a brave serenity, for a very tender reason which forbade such risks.

A bunch of the church's best men got together and agreed that all Arthur needed was rest; that this bright moment was the right one in which to offer him a vacation; that his physician should flatly order him to take it; and that Byington should arrange the matter.

Leonard accepted the task, the physician spoke with startling flatness, and the whole kind plot worked well. Arthur consented to go away up into the hills beyond all the jar of the busy world's unrest.

Isabel was to go with him, and they were to sojourn at some

point where she would still be within prompt reach of medical skill, yet from which he could make long jaunts into the absolute wilds.

Mrs. Morris was far from well when they left, and the day afterward she was seriously ill. That night Ruth sat up with her, and the next day she was worse, yet begged that no telegram be sent to her daughter.

At the close of the day there came a letter from Isabel. It said that Arthur, "already a new man," would start the next morning at dawn for a three days' trip into the wilderness. He went; and he had not been three hours gone when Isabel received a dispatch calling her to her mother. The only day train would leave in a few minutes, and she had the fortune to catch it.

Ruth met her at the station with the blessed word "better." They went up from the town in Ruth's carriage, Martin Kelly driving, who let it be known that though the doctor's name, "moy graciouz!" were signed to the telegram seven times over, the actual painstaker and sender was "Linnard Boyington, whatsomiver!"

Still Ruth called it the doctor's telegram, and said it made no difference who sent it; but she saw Isabel was disturbed. "Well, Martin, Doctor will have to wait on himself to-morrow; Leonard will be out of town."

That evening, alone with her brother, she said, "But I thought you were to be out of town to-morrow."

"No," he replied, "I don't think I'd better."

Another day passed, another came, and Mrs. Morris was still in danger. Isabel wrote Arthur that she would be with him the moment the peril was over, if he needed her; but if he did not, she would stay on for her mother's fuller recovery. Her letter had barely gone when she received a pencilled line brought in to the mountain hotel by a chance messenger and sent on to her, saying he would be out on his tramp five days instead of three. On the fifth day she telegraphed that her mother was getting well so fast that she would come, now, at his word.

The next morning she betrayed to Ruth a glad sense of relief as she showed her a dispatch from Arthur, which read: "Going on another trip to-morrow. Stay till I write."

Ruth repeated it to her father and brother at their noonday meal. Leonard made no comment, but the General asked pleasantly—

"Is she certain he won't come in on this evening's express?" He was discerning more than any one wanted him to.

However, at dusk came the train, took water at the tank, stopped at the station, and passed on, and Arthur did not appear.

"Well, I'll go to bed," blithely spoke the General. "I'm not so old as I used to be, but I'm tired, after writing that letter this afternoon—to Godfrey. Good-night." So he gave fair notice that he had moved in this matter, himself.

"I didn't know father had received a letter from Godfrey," said Ruth, shading her face from the lamp, and lifting to Leonard a smile which implied that it would have been but fair for him to have told her.

"It came the day before Arthur went away," replied Leonard, and Ruth reluctantly chose a new topic.

They rarely had an evening together thus, and with a soft rain falling at the open windows they sat and talked on many themes in what was to them a very talkative way. When something brought up the subject of the late noted trial, Ruth asked her brother how it had first come to him to suspect so unsuspected a man.

His reply was tardy. "Partly," he said, and mused while he spoke, "because I am so unsuspected a man myself."

He looked up with a smile, half play, half pain. "I know what the mind of an unsuspected man is capable of—under pressure."

The questioner looked on him with fond faith, and then, dropping her eyes to her needlework, said, "That wasn't all that prompted you, was it?"

"No," replied the brother, again musing. "I had noticed the singular value of wanton guesswork."

"I thought so," said the sister. Her needle flagged and stopped, and each knew the other's mind was on the implacable divinations of one morbid soul.

Leonard leaned and fingered the needlework,—a worsted slipper, too small for most men, too large for most women. "Is that for him?"

"Yes," apologized Ruth; "it's the thing every clergyman has to incur. But I'm only doing it to help Isabel out; she has the other."

The evening went quickly. When Leonard let down the window sashes and lowered the shades, Ruth, standing by the lamp as if to put out its light, said, "I'll not go up for a moment or two yet."

She sent him an ardent smile across the room and turned to a desk.

XI

HAS IT COME TO THIS?

Ruth wrote to her lover. Her father's keeping secret his receipt of Godfrey's letter until he had mailed its answer, could mean only that the answer was for Godfrey to come home. The General's talk of being tired by the writing of it was a purely expletive irony, for he had written with the brevity of an old soldier to a young sailor; but he had written that trouble was impending, that its source was Arthur, and that the last hope of removing it lay with him, Godfrey.

A line from Ruth, pursuing after this message, would be one steamer behind it all the way, but it would reach the far wanderer before any leave would permit him to start homeward.

So, now, what should she write? If her father had discerned so much more than he had let any one know he had discerned, how about others? How about the kind whose chief joy is ruthless guesswork? That need of haste was one she had overlooked. Wise father!

And yet—haste itself is such a hazardous thing! Ah, if Arthur had come in on that evening express, what to write were an easier question. The minutes sped by; her pen overhung the paper with the opening sentence unfinished, and every moment the thought she kept putting away came back: "Leonard!—Leonard!—Godfrey's summons should go to him from Leonard; and it should flash under the seas, not crawl across them!"—Hark!

She rose and glided to the door through which her brother had gone. There she was startled by the sight of him speeding cautiously down the stair.

On entering his unlighted room Leonard had moved across it to a front window, where, veiled by the chamber's dusk, he stood looking out into a night dimly illumined by the overclouded moon. The Winslow house widened palely among its surrounding trees. The servants' rooms were remote as well as on the farther side, and on the nearer side no lamplight shone. A short way down the street a glow came from the Morris cottage. Evidently Isabel was with her mother.

He stood and mused, unconsciously lulled by the cool drip of myriad leaves, and with his mind poised midway between emotion and thought. To yield to emotion would have been to chafe against the bands that knitted his life and hers to every life about them. To yield to thought would have been to think of her as no more to be drawn from these surrounding ties than some animate rainbow-fringed flower of the sea can be torn from its shell without laceration and death. To give thought word would have been to cry, "Oh, truest of womankind, where would this unsuspected man, this Leonard Byington, be if you were other than you are?" Yet the suspense between avoided feeling and avoided thought held him where he stood.

So standing, it drifted idly into his mind that yonder arbor must be very wet to-night, and the cinder sidewalk out here much drier. As the thought moved him to draw one step back, the glow from the cottage broadened. Its front door had opened, and Mrs. Morris's young maid came out with a lantern, followed by Isabel saying last fond words to her mother as the convalescent closed the door.

"Good-night!" she called back.

In one great wave the young man's passion rolled over its bounds and brought him to his knees with arms outstretched. "Oh, Isabel!" he murmured. "Oh, my God! Oh, Isabel! Isabel! if I had but lost you fairly!"

The two slight figures came daintily along the wet path in single file, the maid throwing the lantern's beams hither and yon as she looked back to answer Isabel's kindly questions; Isabel one moment half lost in the gloom of the trees, and then so lighted up again from foot to brow that it was easy to see the very lines of her winsome mouth, ripe for compassion or fortitude, yet wishful as a little child's.

Her secret observer moaned as he stood erect. The fury of his soul seemed to enhance his stature. He did not speak again, but, "Oh, Isabel! harder to strive against than all the world beside!" was the unuttered cry that wrote itself upon his tortured brow. "If your unfair winner would only hold you by fair means! Yet I too was to blame! I too was to blame, and you alone were blameless!"

Opposite his window Isabel ceased her light talk with the maid, halted, bent, and scanned something just off the firm path, in the clean wet sand.

The maid turned and flooded her with the light of the lantern just as she impulsively lifted an alarmed glance to Leonard's window and as quickly averted it. "Go on," said the mistress. "I can walk faster if you can."

The girl quickened her steps, but had not taken a dozen when Isabel stopped again. "Wait, Minnie. Now you can run back, thank you." She reached for the lantern.

"I—I thought I was to go all the way, and—and bring the lantern back."

"No, I'll keep the lantern; but I'll stay here and throw the light after you till you get in. Run along."

Minnie tripped away. As she came where they had first halted, a purposely belated good-night softly overtook her; and when she looked back, Isabel, as if by inadvertency, sent the lantern's beam into her eyes. So too much light sent the maid by the spot unenlightened.

Leonard drew aside lest the beam swing next into his window. But the precaution was wasted; the glare followed Minnie.

Isabel also followed, slowly, a few paces, and then moved obliquely into the roadway and toward the window. Only for a moment the ray swept near her unseen observer, and, lighting up the rain-packed sand close before herself, revealed a line of footprints slanting toward her from Leonard's own gate.

As the cottage door shut Minnie in, Isabel, reassured by the brightness of the Byingtons' lower windows, stopped for a furtive instant, and holding in her hand the fellow of the slipper so lately in Ruth's fingers, exactly fitted it to one of these footprints. Then, with the lantern on her farther side, and every vein surging with fright and shame, she made haste toward the open gateway of the Winslow house.

A short space from it she recoiled with a gesture of dismay and self-repression, and her light shone full upon a man. He stepped from the garden, his form tensely lifted, his face aflame with anger.

But her small figure straightened also, and swiftly muffling the lantern in a fold of her skirt, she exclaimed, audibly only to him, though in words clear-cut as musical notes, "Oh, Arthur Winslow, has it come to this?"

She arrested his resentful answer by the uplift of a hand, which left the lantern again uncovered. "Inside! In the house!" she softly cried, starting on. "Not here! Look!—those upper windows!— we're in full view of them!"

Quickly she remuffled the lantern, but not in time to hide his motion as he threw out an arm and pushed her rudely back, while he exclaimed, "In full view of them answer me one question!"

It was then that Leonard went hurriedly downstairs.

XII

THE LANTERN QUENCHED

"I will answer you nothing!" murmured Isabel, still facing her husband as she moved round into the garden driveway. "Arthur Winslow, it is you who are on trial, not I!"

"I on trial! God, listen to that!"

He sprang after her, gripped her shoulders, and hung over her, snarling, "You two-faced runaway! what have I done but suffer?"

She kept the lantern hid. "What have you done? Oh, my husband, will you hear if I tell you? You have hung the fates of all of us, living or yet to live, on one thread,—please, dear, don't bear so heavily on me,—on one poor thread which the jar of another misstep will surely break. Oh, let us not make it! Come, Arthur,—my husband,—into the house; maybe we can yet save ourselves and our dear ones! Arthur, you're hurting me dreadfully. If you press me down that way, you'll force me to my knees."

Still she spoke in undertone, and still she muffled the light, while steadily the weight of his arms increased. Suddenly he crowded her to the earth. "Arthur," she murmured, "Arthur, what are you going to do? Don't kill me here and now, Arthur; wait till to-morrow. I have that to pass through to-night which may end my life peaceably in bed; and if it should, then there will be no infamy on any of us,—on you or our child, living, or on me, dead; and Godfrey, and Ruth, and mother, and all can be"—

"Give me that lantern!" He held her with one hand, snatched the light from cover, and thrust it into her face. "So this is what you signal him with, is it?"

"Oh no, no! Arthur, dear, no! Before God's throne, no!"

He lifted it as high as his arm would go, and with all his force swung it down, crashing and quenched, upon her head.

She gave a gentle sigh and rolled at his feet. Groaning with horror and fright, he lifted her in his arms and bore her to her room and bed.

There she presently opened her eyes to find him laving her face and head, moaning, covering them with kisses, and imploring her forgiveness in a thousand hysterical repetitions.

"Hush, dear," she whispered. "I see how it all happened. Does anybody know? Oh, God be thanked! don't let any one find out! It was all a misunderstanding. So many things crowded together to mislead you!"

"Oh yes, so many, many things at once, my treasure! Oh yes, yes!"

"Call Sarah, will you, dear?"

"Oh, beloved, why should I? You don't need Sarah for anything."

"Yes, I need her. I must send her for mother—and Ruth—I promised Ruth; and you must send Giles for the doctor; my hour is come."

In the Byington house Ruth and her brother met at the foot of the stairs.

"Leonard," she whispered, "what is it? Is father ill? Leonard! Oh, what have you seen?"

"Let me pass! quick!" He would have pressed her aside, but she laid hands on him.

"What has Arthur done?" she asked. "What is he doing?"

"Ruth! Ruth! he is putting her out of his own gate!" The brother extended both hands to turn the sister from his path, but she twined her arms on his.

"Leonard! Leonard! for the love of heaven, let him do it! She has only to go to her mother; let her go! It's the last hope. But she'd better be dead, and she'd a hundred times rather be dead, than that Leonard Byington should be her rescuer! Come in here a minute."

Slipping both hands into his she drew him into the lighted room, adding as they went, "In a few minutes I can make some errand to her and find how matters stand"—

They stumbled over a disordered rug. She fell into a chair; he sank to his knees, and with his face in her hands he moaned, "Oh, Ruth! Oh, Ruth! it's my fault after all! I should have gone away at the beginning!"

Ruth and Arthur met face to face in the Winslow garden. "I was just coming for you," he said, excitedly.

"For Isabel?"

"Yes, her mother is with her, and"—a sound of wheels—"here's Giles, now, off for the doctor."

The servant passed. "Yes, I got here by the sunset express. I couldn't stay away—with this impending."

99

"I didn't see you come."

"No, of course you didn't see me, for I didn't go to the station, and so I didn't pass anywhere near your house. I got off at the tank and came up the hill path."

"You must have got drenched; you are drenched."

"Oh no! I got in before the rain began. Let myself in without seeing any one, and found Isabel was over at her mother's. So I waited here."

"Didn't let her know you were home?" asked Ruth, with a penetrating gaze.

"No, I haven't been off the place since I came, but I stepped out so many times into the garden to see if she was coming that I'm soaking wet."

They entered the lighted house, and he turned upon her a glance heavy and wavering with falsehood. His tongue ran like a terrified horse. "Oh—eh—before you go upstairs—Ruth—there's one thing I'm distressed about. I've told Mrs. Morris, and she's promised to see that the doctor understands it perfectly,—though I shall explain it to him myself the moment he comes. And still I wish you'd see that he understands, will you?"

"What is it?"

"Why, at last, as I was waiting for Isabel, and saw her coming, I went to meet her. Unfortunately she took me for a stranger, turned to run, and tripped and fell headlong! She somehow got her lantern between the base of a tree and the crown of her head, smashed the lantern, and cut and bruised her head pitifully!"

To hide her start of distress Ruth moved up the stair; but after a step or two she turned. "Arthur, why say anything about it, if nothing is asked?"

The husband stared at her and turned deadly pale.

"Th—that's tr—true!" he said, with an eager gesture. "I'll not mention it. And—Ruth!"—she was leaving him—"you might s—say the same to Mrs. Morris!"

She nodded, but would not trust her eyes to meet his. He was right; she had divined his deed.

He went loiteringly into the library and gently closed the door. Then he turned the light low, paced once up and down the room, and all at once slammed himself full length upon a lounge, and lay face up, face down, by turns, writhing and tearing his hair.

Soon again he was pacing the floor, and presently was prone once more, and then once more up.

Giles, his English man, brought the doctor, and Arthur heard him discoursing as the vehicle drew up.

"Yes, sir, quite so; quite so, sir. And yet I believe, sir, if h-all money and lands was 'eld in common, the 'ole 'uman ryce would be as 'appy as the gentlemen and lydies on Bylow 'Ill!"

The young husband met the physician cheerily, sent him up, and went back to his solitude.

An hour passed, and then Sarah Stebbens knocked and leaned in. "Mr. Arthur!"

"What, Sarah?"

"Oh! I didn't see you. All's well, and it's a daughter."

XIII

BABY

It was most pleasant, being asked by everyone, even by General Byington, how it felt to be a grandmother. "Oh! ho, ho!" Mrs. Morris's unutilized dimple kept itself busy to the point of positive fatigue.

Even more delightful was it, when the time came round for the totality of her sex—the only sex worth considering—to call and see the babe and mother, to hear them all proclaim it the prettiest infant ever seen, and covertly pronounce Isabel more beautiful than on her wedding day.

In a way she was; and particularly when they fondly rallied her upon her new accession of motherly practical manner, and she laughed with them, and ended with that merry, mellow sigh which still gave Ruth new pride in her and new hope. But another source of Ruth's new hope was that Arthur, who had written to the bishop and resigned his calling the day after Mrs. Morris's little namesake was born, had at length withdrawn his letter.

"It is to your brother we owe its withdrawal," said the bishop, privately, to Ruth.

She beamed gratefully, but did not tell him that, after the long, secret conference between her brother and the rector, Leonard had come to her and wept for Arthur the only tears he had ever shed in her presence. Now Leonard had found occasion to go West for a time, though he still held his office; and Arthur was filling the rectorate almost in the old first way. On some small parish matter the rustic vestryman with the spectacled daughter came to Arthur's library in better spirits than he had shown for months, and by and by asked conjecturally, "I—eh—guess you don't keep any babies here you're ashamed to show, do ye?" and held his mouth very wide open.

The infinitesimal was brought.

"Well, I vum! Why, Miz. Winslow, I don't believe th' ever was a pretty baby so puny, nor a puny baby so pretty! Now, if it's a fair question, I hope y' ain't tryin' to push in between this baby and the keaow, be ye?"

"No," laughed Isabel. "I'm not that conceited. I should only be in the way."

"Well," he said as they parted, shaking Arthur's hand to the end of his speech, "I like to see a baby resemble its father, and that's what this 'n 's a-tryin' to do, jest 's hard 's she can."

So went matters for a time, and then, while the babe began to fill out and lengthen out, Isabel showed herself daily more and more overspent. The physician reappeared, and spoke plainly:—

"And if your cousin down South is so determined to have you at her wedding, why, go! Leave your baby with your mother; she's older in the business than you are."

But the cousin's wedding was weeks away yet, and Isabel clung to her wee treasure, and temporized with the aunts and cousins in the South and with her mother and Ruth at home, until the doctor spoke again.

"Let's see," he said to Arthur. "This is November, baby's five months old. Send your wife away. Put her out! Something's killing her by inches, and I believe it's just care o' the nest. We must drive her off it, as I drove Leonard Byington off,—which, you remember, you, quietly, were the first to suggest to me to do.... Coming back, you say,—Byington? Yes, but only for a day or two,—election time."

It did not occur to the doctor that Arthur was secretly keeping his wife from going anywhere.

The night Leonard came home the old pond, for the first time in the season, froze over, and through Giles's activities it was arranged next day that Martin Kelly, Sarah Stebbens, Minnie, and he should go down there after supper and skate by the light of fagot fires made out on the ice. Giles piled the fagots; but at a late moment, to the disgust of Giles and Minnie, the older pair pitilessly changed their minds, and decided they were too old to make such nincompoops of themselves. Minnie would not go without Sarah, for Minnie was up to her pretty eyebrows in love with Giles, as well as immensely correct; and so there, as it seemed, was the end of that.

At tea Arthur told Isabel he was going for a long walk down through the town and across the meadows, and would not be home before bedtime. Isabel approved heartily, and said Sarah would stay near the sleeping babe, and she would spend the evening with her mother. She and Arthur went together as far as the cross-paths in the arbor, and there, in parting, he clasped and kissed her with a sudden frenzy that only added one more distressful misgiving to the many that now haunted her days.

103

She found her mother alone. They sat down, hand in hand, before an open fire, and had talked in sweet quietness but a short while, when a chance word and the knowledge that this time they would not be interrupted made it easy for Isabel to say things she had for weeks been trying to say.

XIV

THE TALKATIVE LEONARD

Across the street the father of Leonard and Ruth, already abed, lay thinking of their tribulation and casting about in his mind for some new move that might help to end it happily. Godfrey had not come. He had not looked for him to appear with a hop, skip, and a jump, "a man under authority" as he was; but here were five months gone.

"I can't clamor for him," thought he, and feared Ruth had written him that the emergency was past. And so she had, in those days of new hope and new suspense which had followed for a while Arthur's withdrawal of his resignation.

At the fireside below sat Leonard and Ruth, not hand in hand, like Isabel and her mother, yet conversing on the same theme as they.

Leonard had spent the day at the polls; his party had won an easy victory; and, though not on the ticket, he was now awaiting a telegraphic summons to the state capital. His fortunes were growing. Yet that was not a thing to be wordy about, and now, when the murmur of his voice continued so long and steadily that it found even the dulled ear of the aged father in the upper room, that father knew what the topic must be. On all other matters the son and brother had become more silent than ever,—was being nicknamed far and near, flatteringly and otherwise, for his reticence; but let Ruth sit down with him alone and barely draw near this theme,— this wound,—and his speech bled from him and would not be stanched.

"I can admit I have made the mistake of my life," he said, "but I cannot and will not, even now, give up and say there is nothing to be saved out of it. It's a mistake that has bound me to her, to you, to Godfrey, to him, to all, and demands of me, pinioned and blindfolded as I am, every effort I can make, every device I can contrive, to compel him to free her and you and all of us from this torture.

105

"He shall not go on eating out our lives. I have dawdled with him weakly, pitifully, but I did it in my hope to save him. I tried to save him for his own sake, Ruth, truly,—as truly as for her sake and ours; and I wanted to save his work with him,—his church, his and hers; so much of it is hers. Oh, Ruth, I love that little bird-box, spite of all its spunky beliefs and twittering complacencies. I wanted to save it and him; and over and over there has seemed such good ground of hope in him. It's been always so unbelievable that he should utterly fail us. Ruth, if you could have seen his contrition the night I tore up that shameful, servile resignation! I don't need to see Isabel to know he is wearing the soul out of her. You needn't have answered one of my questions,—which I honor you for answering so unwillingly; Mrs. Morris gave me their answer in five minutes, though we talked only of investments. And Mrs. Morris needn't have given it; to see Arthur himself is enough. All the genuineness has gone out of the man,—out of his words, out of his face, out of his voice. I wonder it hasn't gone from all of us, driven out by this smirking masquerade into which he has trapped us."

"Have you determined what to do?" asked the sister, gazing into the fire.

"Not yet. But I sha'n't go back West. Flight doesn't avail. And, Ruth"—

"Yes, brother; you've cabled?"

"I have. He'll come at once, this time." A step on the porch drew the speaker to the door.

The telegram from the capital had come. But until its bearer had gone again and was out of hearing down the street the young man lingered in the porch. His mind was wholly on that evening when Isabel had passed with the lantern. Would she pass now? From the idle query he turned to go in, when Ruth came out, and they stayed another moment together. Presently their ear caught a stir at the side of the Morris cottage.

"Hmm," murmured Ruth half consciously, and, with a playful shudder at the cold, whispered, "Come in, come in!"

But then quickly, lest this should carry a hint of distrust, she tripped in alone, closed the door, and glided to the bright hearth. There a moment of waiting changed her mind. She ran again to the door, and began to say as she threw it open, "My brother! you'll catch your"—

But no brother was there.

XV

THE THIN ICE BREAKS

Isabel, who had never confessed her trouble to her mother until now, had this evening told all there was to tell.

"No, no, my dear," she said as she moved to go, "I have no dread of his blows. I don't suppose he will ever strike me again. Ah, there's the worst of it; he's got away, away beyond blows. I wish sometimes he'd brain me, if only that would stop his secretly watching me.

"If he'd never gone beyond blows, I would have died before I would have told; not for meekness, dearie, nor even for love,—of you, or my child, or any one,—but just for pride and shame. But to know, every day and hour, that I'm watched, and that every path I tread is full of traps,—there's what's killing me. And I could let it kill me and never tell, if being killed were all. But I tell you because— Oh, my poor little mother dearie, do I wear you out, saying the same things over and over?

"This is all I ask you to remember: that my reason for telling you is to save the honor of my husband himself, and of you, dear heart, and of—of my child, you know. For, mother, every innocent thing I do is being woven into a net of criminating evidence. Sooner or later it's certain to catch me fast and give me over, you and me and—and baby, to public shame."

As they went toward the arbor door Isabel warily hushed, but her mother said: "There's no one to overhear, honey-blossom; Minnie's at your house with Sarah."

But neither was there more to be said. The daughter shut herself out, and stood alone on the doorstep pondering what she had done. For she had acted as well as spoken, and, without knowledge of Leonard's move, was calling Godfrey home herself. Her mother was to send the dispatch in the morning.

So standing and distressfully musing, she heard the click of the Byingtons' door as Ruth left Leonard on the porch. But her thought went after Arthur. Where was he? That he had honestly gone where he had said he was going she painfully doubted. She

107

stirred to move on, but had not taken a step when a feminine cry of terror set her blood leaping and sent her flying down the arbor, and where the two paths crossed she and Leonard met at such a speed that only by seizing her with both his hands did he avoid trampling her down. The scream was repeated again and again.

"It's Minnie!" cried Isabel as they sprang down the path to the mill pond; and Leonard, outrunning her, called back,—

"We'll get her out! She's not gone under!"

The next moment he, and then she, were on the scene. Minnie stood on the firmer ice away from the bank, moaning in continued agitation, but already rescued. It was Arthur Winslow who had saved her.

Now he gained the bank with the dripping girl, where he yielded her to his wife, and without a word from him, from Isabel, or from Leonard to any one but the incessantly talking maid, the four hurried up the path. When they reached the arbor Ruth had joined them, and there the three women turned to the cottage. Leonard passed on toward his home. Arthur went into his own house.

In the cottage, while being hurried into dry clothes, Minnie more coherently explained her mishap. Wishing to play a joke on Giles, she had slipped away from the fireside company of him and Sarah to put a match to his fagots on the pond, run back with word that they were burning, and laugh with Sarah while Giles should plunge out to find the incendiaries. But she had forgotten how frail good ice may be against a warm bank, and leaping down, had promptly broken through. She had had the fortune to hold on by the ice's outer edge until Arthur, whom she felt sure only Providence could have sent there, drew her out. She was tearfully ashamed, yet not so broken in spirit but she fiercely vowed she would get even with Giles for this yet.

Leonard went to his room, Arthur to his, and each in his way shut himself in to darkness, silence, and the fury of his own heart.

One of the things most harrowing to Leonard was that, at every turn, the active part fell to Arthur, while him fate held mercilessly to the passive; and his soul writhed in unworded prayer for any conceivable turn of events that would give him leave to act, to do!

But all he could do was done. Godfrey was sent for: everything must await his coming. Heaven hold Arthur's hand till Godfrey could come!

Ruth returned home and began to lock up the house. When,

presently, she tapped at her brother's door and looked in, he had lighted the room and was reading his telegram.

"All right over the way," she said, and to hurry on over the grim untruth repeated briefly Minnie's story. "Good-night. You go—to-morrow? Well, you'll make haste back."

She left him, but later returned.

"Leonard." At the slightly opened door she thrust in her Bible, with a finger on the line, "My soul, wait thou only upon God."

"Thank you," said the brother. "Good-night. I'm afraid we've kept Him waiting on us."

XVI

MUST GIVE YOU UP

Over on the Winslow side of the way, Isabel, having tarried in the cottage to explain to her frightened mother how perfectly natural it was that Arthur, after his tramp across the meadows, should have made a circuit to the upper side of the old mill pool, went pensively home. Presently, holding a lamp, she stood in the door between her room and Arthur's, lifted the light above her head, and, shading her brows, called his name. Hidden in the gloom, silent and motionless, he stared for a moment on the beautiful apparition, and then moved without a sound into the beams of the lamp, a picture of misery and desperation.

"Why in the dark?" amiably inquired the wife.

With widening eyes and spectral motions he drew near.

"In the dark?" he asked. "Why in the dark? The darkness is in me, and all the lamps that light the world's ships into harbor could not dispel it."

All at once he went to his knees. "Oh, my wife, my wife! save me, save me! Hell is in my soul!"

She drew back, and with low vehemence urged him to his feet. "Up! up! My husband shall not kneel to me!"

Laying her hand reverently upon his shoulder she pressed him into his room, set the lamp aside, and let him clasp her wildly in his arms.

"Save me, Isabel," he moaned again. "Save me."

"From what, dear heart,—from what can I save you?" She drew him to a seat and knelt beside him.

"From the green-eyed demon that has gnawed, gnawed, gnawed at my heart till it is rent to shreds, and at my brain—my brain!—till it is almost gone." His brow drooped to hers. "Almost gone, beloved; my brain is almost gone."

"No, Arthur, dearest, no, no, no; your heart is torn, but your mind, thank God, is whole. This is only a mood. Come, it will pass with one night's sleep."

110

Still he held her brow beneath his. "Save me, Isabel; my soul is almost gone. Oh, save me from the fiends that come before me and behind me, by night and by day, eyes shut or eyes open."

"My husband! my love! how can I save you? How can I help you? Tell me how."

"Hear me! hear me confess! That will save me, oh, so sweetly, so sweetly! That will save me from the faces—the white, white faces that float on that black pool down yonder, and move their accusing lips at me: his face—and mine—and thine. Oh, Isabel, until you stood before me in the golden light of your lamp, transfigured into a messenger from heaven, it was in my lost soul to do the deed this night."

The wife laid her palms upon her husband's temples, and putting forth her strength lifted them and looked tenderly into his eyes.

"Dear heart, you do not frighten me. You know how unaccountably fear deserts me in fearful moments. But I know there's nothing for either of us to fear now. This is all in your tortured imagination, and there, though you had not seen me, it would have stayed; you never would have come to the act. Arthur, your soul is not lost. You who have pointed the way of escape and deliverance so clearly and savingly to so many, you need not miss it now yourself."

"Idle words, Isabel,—idle, idle words. The very words of Christ are idle to me until I give you up."

"Give me up, my husband? Dear love, you cannot! You shall not! I will not be given up. You haven't the cause, and I haven't the cause."

"Oh, Isabel, I stole you! And the curse of God has gone with the theft, and with every step of the thief, from the first day till now. From the first day until now God has lifted that other man up and brought me down. And yet, before God who said, Thou shalt not covet thy neighbor's wife, he loves you this moment—now!—with the love of a man for a woman."

"Arthur, no! If he did"—

"Isabel, if he did not—if he did not love you yet as before he lost you—oh! if he did not love you infinitely more now than then— he would not be Leonard Byington. That is all my evidence, all my argument, all the ground of my hate; and I hate him with a hatred that has finished—finished!—with my heart, and is devouring my brain."

"Oh, my poor husband, listen to"—

"Listen to me!" he broke in. "Listen before I lose the blessed

111

impulse to say there is but one cure. I must give you up to Leonard Byington. Oh, let me speak! I took you from him by law; by law I will give you back."

"Do you mean divorce, Arthur?"

"I do."

"On what ground?"

"On the ground of ill treatment. You shall bring suit; I will plead guilty."

She rose, with his temples still in her hands. "Ah! whose words are idle now?"

She bent over him with eyes of passionate kindness. "You did not take me from him. You asked me to take you, and for better for worse, till death us do part, I took you, Arthur, knowing as much of any other man's love for me as I know at this hour. You could not steal me; the shame would be mine, to have let you. You are no thief! I am no stolen thing! You shall be happy with me; you shall not give me up!"

He leaped to his feet and snatched her into his arms. The babe cried sleepily from its mother's room. She tenderly disengaged herself, left him in the door, moved on to the child's crib, and in the dim light of the bedside taper, facing him from beyond it, soothed the little one by her silent touch.

To Arthur, wan and frail though she was, the sight was heavenly fair, a vision of ineffable peace to which it seemed a sacrilege to draw nearer; but she beckoned, and he stole to the spot. With the quieted babe in its crib between them, the pair knit arms about each other's neck and kissed.

"My own! my own at last!" murmured the husband. "I never had you until now!"

"The cure has worked, dear heart," breathed the wife,—"worked without surgery, has it not?"

"The cure has worked," he replied,—"worked without the sacrifice. Oh, the sudden sweet ease of it!"

Whispering a fervent good-night in response to hers, he covered her head and brows with caresses; then stole away with eyes still fastened on her, and at the dividing threshold waved a last parting and closed the door.

XVII

SLEEP, OF A SORT

Isabel went to her couch in great heaviness and agitation. Her sad confidings to her mother, Minnie's adventure, Arthur's pitiful if not alarming condition, she strove to reconsider duly and in their order; but perpetually there interfered, with its every smallest detail thrillingly clear and strong, that moment which had thrown her once more into the company, tossed her into the very clutch, of Leonard Byington. She turned her face into her pillow and prayed God for other thoughts and visions, and at length, while charging herself to see her mother in time to postpone the sending of her dispatch to Godfrey, she slept.

Sleep, of a sort, came also to Arthur, though not before many an evil imagination had come back to tease and sting his galled mind.

What chafed oftenest was the fact that Isabel, had he allowed it, would have sought to argue down his belief that Leonard loved her. Great heaven! what must be her feeling toward him, that she should offer to argue such a question? She might truly deny all knowledge of his passion, but oh, where were her quick outcries of womanly abhorrence? Where was the word that Leonard Byington was no more to her than any other man,—that word which would have been the first to flash from her if conscience had not stopped it? Twice he sprang up in his bed, whispering: "They love! They love! Each knows it of the other! They love!"

The second time, as he stared, suddenly he saw them! They stood just beyond the foot of his couch, wrapped in each other's arms. Choking with wrath, freezing with horror, he slid to the floor; but at his first step they floated apart. Isabel glided toward her own door, fading as she went, and dissolved in a broad moonbeam. Leonard, as he receded, grew every instant more real, until, at his pursuer's second step, he melted through a window and was gone. Arthur sprang to the spot and stared out and down; but all he saw was the moon, the frosty night, and the silent, motionless garden.

113

With a whisper of fierce purpose he turned and noiselessly threw on his clothes, then clutched his head in his hands in a wild effort to recall what the purpose was, and by and by lay quietly down again on his bed. He could not recollect; but the inner tumult quieted more and more, and after a time, without putting off any part of his dress, he drew the bedcovers over himself, and in a few moments was partially asleep. So for an hour or more he lay in half-waking dreams, ghastly with phantoms and breathless with dismay of his own ferocious strivings. Then he rose once more, and, with the noiselessness which habit had perfected, left his room, moved down the upper hall and the stair, and let himself out into the garden. Wadded in his arms he bore one or two of the coverings from his bed. He took his way to the pond.

He was walking in his sleep.

At an earlier day Isabel would have been awakened by her husband's softest movement; but now, used to his stirrings, weary in body and mind, and in some degree reassured, she slept on unstartled until Arthur's return.

He came as silently as he had gone, and was empty-handed. He had tied a great stone in the two bed-coverings, and through the thin new ice of the hole where Minnie had broken in had sunk them in the black depth under the shelving rock. He was still asleep.

The door between the two chambers gave a faint sound as he opened it, yet neither mother nor child moved. A moment passed, and he had reached the bed. Another went by, and Isabel was awake, wildly but vainly trying to scream, to rise. A knee was on her bosom, two hands grappled her throat, and two out-starting eyes were close to hers. Her husband was strangling her.

Then he too awoke. With a horrified cry he recoiled, and she, for the first time in her life in a transport of terror, hurled him, in the strength of her frenzy, to the farther side of the bed, and writhing out on the opposite side, crept under it and lay still. In a torture of bewilderment and remorse Arthur buried his face in the bedside. Then, helpless to distinguish what he had done from what he had dreamed, he sprang back to the place where Isabel had lain sleeping, and lo, it was empty.

"Oh, was it thou, was it thou?" he wailed, in a stifled voice. "Was it not he?"

Whispering and moaning her name, hearkening and groping, he sought her from corner to corner, first of her room and then of his own, and then went to the hall and to other rooms in the same harrowing quest.

Isabel crept forth and darted to her babe. Yet as she leaned to

114

take it in her arms her better judgment told her the child was safe. The husband too, and every one beside, were safer from his jealous wrath while the babe remained. With one anguished knitting of her hands over it she left it, and fled in her night-dress. Arthur's course was made plain by his moanings, and easily avoiding him, she glided down a back stair, out into the arbor, and across to her mother's cottage and bed-chamber. As she did so he returned hurriedly to his room, with low cries of less wretched conviction, and looked eagerly under his bed and then under hers. Thereupon the last hope died, and he dropped to his face on the floor in abject agony.

XVIII

MISSING

After a time a new conjecture brought him to his feet. To solve it he would go to the pond. If he had truly been there and done this appalling thing, he would know it by the empty imprint of the boulder he had taken from its resting place of years. If he had not, then Isabel had fled to her mother and would be found with her in the morning, and the blot of her murder, though it blackened his soul, was yet not on his hands.

He went to the water, and soon he came again with the step and face of one called out of his grave. Slowly he counted the disordered coverings of his wife's couch, stood a moment in desolate perplexity, and then went quickly and counted those of his own. A sheet and a blanket were gone. He turned to a closet and supplied the lack, and then paced the floor until dawn.

Before the servants were fairly astir he laid away the clothing Isabel had put off, and contrived to leave the house and pass through the arbor unseen until he reached its farther end; but there Mrs. Morris, in a dressing gown, opened to him before he could knock. She forced her usual laugh, but he saw the white preparedness of her face.

"She knows my crime," he thought, and was in agony to guess how she had got the knowledge and what she would do with it.

"Why, Arthur," she sweetly began, "what brings you"—But her throat closed.

"Mother," he interrupted emotionally as they shut themselves in, "is Isabel here?"

"Isabel?—No-o! Why—why, Arthur, she went home last night before ten o'clock!" The little lady knew her acting was not good, but it was better than she had hoped to make it. "Arthur Winslow! don't tell me my child is not at home! Oh, my heavens!"

"Wait, mother; listen. I beseech you. Do you absolutely know she's not here?"

"I know it! Oh, Arthur, are you only trying to break bad news to me by littles? Has Isabel destroyed herself? Has she fled?" The inquirer played well now; her pallor, that had seemed to accuse him, was gone, and her question offered a cue which he greedily took.

"Fled? Isabel! Destroyed herself,—that spotless soul? Oh no, no, no! But Oh merciful God! I am afraid she has been stolen!" He sank into a seat and dropped his face into his hands.

The maid's steps sounded overhead, and he started up. Mrs. Morris laid a hand on his arm. She was pale again, but her words were reassuring.

"It's Minnie," she murmured: "let me go and see her. She'll not be surprised; I'm always the first one up." She went, and was soon back again.

"There is no time to lose"—Arthur began.

"No, you must go. Go search for every clue that will tell us a word of her; but, whatever you do, let no one, not even Sarah, know she is missing, until we know enough ourselves to protect her from every shadow of reproach!"

"True! true! right! right!" said Arthur, while with secret terror he cried to himself: "This woman knows! She knows, she knows, and all this is make-believe, put on to gain time!"

But he saw no safer course than to help on the sham. "Right," he said again; "only, mother, dear, how shall we hide her absence?"

"We needn't hide it. You know she got another telegram last night, begging her to come at once to the wedding. We can say she went on this morning's train, before day; it makes such good Southern connections. And now go! make your search with all your might! and after a while I'll come over and pack a trunk full of her things, and express it South, just as if she were there, and had gone so hurriedly that—Don't you see?"

Arthur said he saw it all, but he did not; he saw much that was not, and much that was he saw not. He did not see that the dust of the old street, and of the new town as well, was on Mrs. Morris's shoes; and that Isabel, in a gown which she had left at the cottage when she went to be mistress of his home, was really on the train, bound South.

Dropping all pretence of having any search to make, he hurried back to his own room, and by and by told the pleasantly astonished Sarah and Giles the simple truth as Mrs. Morris had put it into his mouth, but told it in the firm belief that he was covering a hideous crime with an all but transparent lie.

After a false show of breakfasting he went into his study,—"to work on his sermon," he said; but did nothing there but pace the floor, hold his head, and whisper, "It will not last an hour after he has heard it," and, "O God, have mercy! Oh, my wife, my wife! Oh, my brain, my brain!"

XIX

A DOUBLE STILL HUNT

Mrs. Morris's task was too large for her. She had always taken such care of her innocence that her cultivation of the virtues had been only incidental. Hence, morally, she had more fat than fibre; and hence again, though to her mind guilt was horrible, publicity was so much worse that her first and ruling impulse toward any evil doing not her own was to conceal it. That was her form of worldliness, the only fault she felt certain she was free from. And here she was, without a helping hand or a word of counsel, laboring to hide from the servants and from the dear Byingtons, from the church and from a scoffing world, the hideous fact that Isabel was a fugitive from the murderous wrath of a jealous husband, and that the rector of All Angels had crumbled into moral ruin.

"And oh," she cried, "is it the worst of it, or is it the best of it, that in this awful extremity he keeps so sane, so marvellously sane?" She said this the oftener because every few hours some new sign to the contrary forced itself upon her notice. Oblivion was her cure-all.

For a while after his conference with Mrs. Morris Arthur made some feeble show—for her eye alone—of looking after clews, and then, as much to her joy as to her amazement, told her it was a part of his detective strategy to return into his study, and seemingly to his ordinary work, until time would allow certain unfoldings for which he looked with confidence.

"Have you found out anything?" she asked, with a glaringly false eagerness that gave him a new panic of suspicion and whetted his cunning.

He said he had, but must beg her not to ask yet what it was. Then he inquired if any neighbor had left town that morning for Boston, and her heart rose into her throat as she marked the subtlety he could not keep out of his dark face.

"Why, ye—yes—n—no, no one that I know of ex—except Leonard Byington," she replied, and thought, "If he should accuse Leonard, we are undone!"

To avoid that risk she would have told him, then and there, all she knew, had she not feared she might draw his rage upon herself for aiding the wife's flight. She must, must, must keep on good terms with him till she and Isabel could somehow get the child. So passed the awful hours, mother and husband each marvelling in agony over the ghastly puzzle of the other's apathy.

Later in the day she knocked timorously at his study door. She had come with a silly little proposition that he let her take the infant and go South as if to join Isabel. Thus the trunk would not lie in the express office down there, unclaimed and breeding awkward inquiries, and she from that point, with him at this, could keep up the illusion they had invented until Isabel herself should—eh— return!

But when he let her in, he stood before her a silent embodiment of such remorse and foreboding that she could have burst into sobs and cries.

Yet she broached her plan, trembling visibly, while he heard her through with melancholy deference.

In reply he commended it, but called to her notice how much better it would be for her to go alone. Then the babe, left behind, would be an unspoken yet most eloquent guarantee that its mother would soon reappear.

"Very true," responded the emboldened lady; "yet on the other hand"—

He put out an interrupting touch. "The child is as safe with me as if it were in its mother's bosom."

"Oh, it isn't so much a question of safety as"—

The father interrupted again, with a gleam in his eyes like the outflashing of a knife. "I hold the child against all comers, and would if I had to slay its mother to do it."

Mrs. Morris stifled an outcry and would have left him, but he would not let her.

"Stay! Oh, listen to a soul in torment! The babe is already motherless. Isabel can never return, mother; she is with the dead. I am not waiting idly here for her; I am waiting busily—for her slayer. He has fled; but when he sees he is not pursued he will come back to the spot,—to the black, black hole. He cannot help it. I know that. Oh, how well I know it! And the moment he comes he is caught,— caught in the web of proofs I am weaving!"

He held her arm and gazed into her gazing eyes in ferocious fear of the web she might be weaving for him; while she, reeling sick with fear of him, tried with all her shaken wits to sham an impassioned accord.

"And you will wait?" she exclaimed approvingly. "You will not stir till the thing is sure?"

He would not stir till the thing was sure.

As soon as it was dark enough to slip over to the Byingtons' unseen, she went, bearing to Ruth Isabel's apologetic good-bys, trying her small best to play at words with the General, and quickly getting away again, grateful for a breath of their atmosphere, though distressfully convinced that Ruth had divined the whole trouble, through the joy betrayed by herself on hearing that Leonard would be away for a week.

She went home and slept like a weary child, and neither the next day nor the next, nor the next, was so awful as this first had been; they lacked the crackle and glare, and the crash, of the burning and falling temple.

XX

A DOUBLE RETURN

Let us not attempt the picture of Isabel keeping the happy guise of a wedding guest among her kindred and childhood playmates while her heart burned with perpetual misery, yearning, and alarm. "My baby, my baby!" cried her breast, while the babe slept sweetly under faultless care.

Nor need we draw a close portrait of her husband's mind, if mind it could longer be called. A horror of sleep, a horror of being awake and aware, remorse, phantoms, voices, sudden blazings of wrath as suddenly gone, sweating panics, that craven care of life which springs so rank as the soul decays, and a steady, cunning determination to keep whole the emptied shell of reputation and rank,—these were the things that filled his hours by day, by night; these, and a frightful expectance of one accusing, child-claiming ghost that never came. The air softened to Indian summer; the ice faded off the pool; a million leaves, crimson and bronze, scarlet and gold, dropped tenderly upon its silvering breadth and lay still; and both the joyless master of the larger house and the merry maid of the cottage asked Heaven impatiently if the pond would never freeze over again.

It was Saturday afternoon when Giles, asked by Sarah Stebbens where Mr. Arthur was, told her he was again, as he had been so many times the last three days, down by the water, sitting at the edge of the overhanging bank; or, as the Englishman expressed it, "'dreamink the 'appy hours aw'y.'" So the week passed out; a second came in, and the rector of All Angels went to his sacred office.

He knew, before he appeared in the chancel, that Mrs. Morris was in her accustomed place, and Ruth and her father in theirs, and that Leonard was not yet reported back nor looked for; but exactly as he began to read, "'Dearly beloved brethren, the Scripture moveth us, in sundry places, to acknowledge and confess our manifold sins and wickedness, and that we should not dissemble

121

nor cloak them before the face of Almighty God our heavenly Father'"—a sickness filled Mrs. Morris's frame, a deathly hue overspread the minister's face, and Leonard came in and sat beside his father and sister.

Yet the service went on. The people knelt.

"'Almighty and most merciful Father; We have erred, and strayed from thy ways like lost sheep. We have followed too much the devices and desires of our own hearts'"—

Thus far the rector's voice had led, but here it sank, and the old General's, in a measure, took its place.

Then it rose again, in the confession, "There is no health in us," and in the supplication, "Have mercy upon us, miserable offenders."

There once more it failed, while the people, faltering with distress, repeated, "That we may hereafter lead a godly, righteous, and sober life, To the glory of thy holy Name. Amen."

At this the farmer with the spectacled daughter stepped nimbly over the rail and caught Arthur as he rose and staggered. Leonard was hurrying forward, and half the people kneeling, half standing, when Mrs. Morris vacantly stopped his way with a face so aghast and words so confused that he had to give her over to Ruth. Then he hastened on to where Arthur was being led into the vestry by his physician and others.

But now he was turned back by the doctor, requesting him to dismiss the congregation; which he did, with the physician's assurance that the trouble was no more than vertigo, and that Arthur was even now quite able to proceed home in the farmer vestryman's rockaway. The people noticed that the physician went with him.

Mrs. Morris followed on foot with the farmer's daughter, and with Ruth and the General, and Leonard went into town to telegraph Isabel, in her mother's name, to come home. As he was starting, Mrs. Morris drew Ruth aside and whispered something about Godfrey. To which Ruth softly replied, with an affectionate twist in her smile, "It couldn't hurry him; he's already on the way."

In the room next that in which her son-in-law lay asleep under anodynes the little mother's odd laugh was turned all to moan. "Oh!—ho—ho!" she sighed in solitude, "if Arthur could have learned from Godfrey how to wait, or even if Isabel could but have learned from Ruth how to keep one waiting!"

She paused at a window that looked over the garden and into the street. Leonard passed. She turned quickly away, only sighing again, "Oh!—ho—ho!" Her thought might have been kinder had she

122

known he was stabbing himself at every step with blame of all this woe.

"I ought to have foreseen," was his constant silent cry. "I am the one who ought to have foreseen."

Lack of Sunday trains and two failures to connect kept Isabel from arriving until nightfall of the third day, Wednesday. Arthur knew Mrs. Morris had telegraphed for her; but to him that was only part of the play under which he thought he and she were hiding the frightful truth.

On this day he had so outwitted his village physician as to be given the freedom for which he ravened; liberty to take the air in his garden, as understood by the doctor, but by him liberty to stand guard down at the edge of that dark pool which would not freeze over,—liberty to take an air sweet with the odors of the parting year, but crowded also with distended eyes and strangling groans.

He was down there in the early starlight when Ruth drove softly into the garden, bringing Isabel. Warily the mother came out into the pillared porch, and silently received the house's mistress into her arms.

"He doesn't know," she said. "I couldn't tell him till you should come, for fear of disappointing him."

The argument seemed strained, but no one said so, and with a whispered good-night Ruth drove away, and the two went in. As they stole upstairs they debated how Isabel had best reveal herself. "I'm terribly afraid that won't work, blessing," said Mrs. Morris; "you'd better let me break it to him, first."

"No, dearie, I don't think so. I haven't the shadow of a fear"—

"Oh, my darling child, you never have!"

"But I know him so well, mother. We have only to come unexpectedly face to face and—Oh, I've seen the effect so often!" They entered her room whispering: "I'll change this dress for the one he last saw me in, and stand over here by the crib where I stood then, and—Oh, sweet Heaven! is this my little flower sleeping just as I left her?" With clasped hands and tearful eyes she bent over the child.

XXI

EVENING RED

Then she began to unrobe, but stopped to throw her arms about her mother's neck.

"Now, dearly beloved, you hurry away down the path and persuade him up and send him in. I'm only afraid you'll find him chilled half to death, it's growing cold so fast. And you can follow in after him, dearie, if you wish,—only not too close."

The mother went, and had got no farther than the cross-path when she came all at once upon the master of the house.

"Oh! ho, ho! here you are! I was just—Arthur, dear, where is your overcoat? Do go right up to your room, my son, till I can get Sarah to have a fire started in the library." She multiplied words in pure affright, so drawn was his face with anguish, and so wild his eyes with aimless consternation.

Without reply he passed in and went upstairs. Mrs. Morris remained below.

Isabel's heart beat fast. She had made her change of dress, and in a far corner of her room, with her face toward the open door that let into his, was again leaning with a mother's ecstasy over the sleeping babe, when she heard his step.

It came to his outer door, which from her place could not be seen.

Did he stop, and stand there? No, he had not stopped; he was only moving softly, for the child's sake.

She stood motionless, listening and looking with her whole soul, and wishing the light were less dim in this shadowy corner, but knowing there was enough to show her to him when he should reach the nearer door. The endless moment wore away, and there on the threshold he stood—if that—Oh merciful God!—if that was Arthur Winslow.

His eyes fell instantly upon her, yet he made neither motion nor sound, only stayed and stared, while an unearthly terror came into his face.

Care of the child kept her silent, but in solemn tenderness she lifted her arms toward him.

He uttered a freezing shriek and fled. In an instant his tread was resounding in the hall, then on two or three steps of the stair as she hurried after, and then there came a long, tumbling fall, her mother's wail in the hail below, and a hoarse cry of dismay from Giles as he rushed out of the library.

"He's only stunned, mum," Giles was saying as Isabel reached the spot. "He's no more nor just stunned, mum."

He had lifted the fallen man's head and shoulders, and Mrs. Stebbens came, dropping to her knees and sprinkling water into the still, white face.

Isabel threw herself between.

"Arthur! Arthur! can't you speak? Oh, let us move him into the library!"

"Yes, um!" exclaimed Giles. "'E'll come to in there; you can see 'e's only stunned."

He tried to raise him, and Isabel and Sarah moved to help; but the wife turned on hearing Ruth's voice at her side, and Leonard Byington lifted the limp man in his arms unaided, and bore him to the library lounge.

"Arthur," he pleaded, with arms still under him, "can't you speak to us, dear boy? Say at least good-by, can't you, Arthur?" He parted the clothing from neck and breast, and laid an ear to his heart.

"Do you hear it, Leonard?" cried the wife. "Oh, you do hear it, don't you, Leonard?"

There was no answer. For a moment Leonard's own form relaxed, and he turned his face and buried it in the unresponsive breast. Then he lifted it again, and taking the other face between his hands he sank his brow to the brow upturned and cried: "God rest your soul, Arthur! Oh, Arthur, Arthur, God rest your soul!"

XXII

MORNING GRAY

Mrs. Morris gave the physician her account of the accident, the physician gave the reporters his, and no other ever got into the old street or the town it looks down upon with such sweet superiority.

Said the rustic vestryman to another pall-bearer, as they turned toward their homes, "Many's the time All Angels's been craowded, but I never see it craowded as 'twas this time."

The new mound was white under January snows when Godfrey and Isabel first stood beside it together; and when summer had come and gone again, and at last the time drew near when, by the regular alternations of the service, the ocean wanderer's three years afloat were to be followed by three ashore, it was beside that mound that Ruth let him ask the long-withheld question.

And once more the new year followed the old.

On one of its earliest days, "I cal'late," a certain somebody began to say to General Byington, "th' never was a happier weddin' so quiet, nor a qui—" But he caught the sheen of his daughter's spectacles and forebore.

And still moved on the heavenly procession of the seasons; and as each new one passed with smile and song, and strewed its flowers or fruits on Bylow Hill, the memory of one who after life's fitful fever slept soundly at last was ever a sweet forgetting of all that had once been bitter, and a sweeter and sweeter remembrance of whatsoever things had been pure, lovely, and of good report.

One day the travelling salesman of fruit trees came again. This time he met Minnie, some of whose information puzzled him.

"But I thought you said the young Mrs. Winslow lived in the large house on this side."

"Yes, but that's the other one; that's Mrs. Isabel Winslow, the widow. Captain Winslow, he's so much o' the time to the navy yard that him and his wife they just keep their home along with her father and Mr. Leonard."

126

"And who is it that, I understand, a Mr. Giles over here is about to marry?"

For reply Minnie covered her mouth and nose with her hand, sputtered, and shut the door in his face.

Another year went by, yet another followed, and still Ruth—daughter, sister, wife, and mother—remained the happy mistress of the house in which she was born, and Leonard remained one of her household. Mrs. Morris turned the cottage over to Mr. and Mrs. Giles—hem!—and dwelt in the Winslow house with Isabel; who, even the young said, grew more beautiful and lovable all the time.

But there came a day, after all,—year uncertain,—when Leonard, with Mrs. Morris's little namesake on his knee, asked Isabel if she did not think it would be well for him to go away for a while; and Isabel murmured no.

So by and by the Winslow pair went to live in the Winslow house, and the Byington pair in the Byington house; and if you listen well, you may hear an aged voice, a voice with a brogue, saying:—

"Ay! there's a Linnard Winslow, now, and there's a Godfrey Boyington. And there's still an Isable Winslow and a Ruth Boyington. But the mother of Ruth Boyington is she that wor Isable Winslow, moy graciouz! and the mother of Isable Winslow is she that wor Ruth Boyington. And so there be's an Isable in the wan house and an Isable in th' other; and there be's a Ruth in the wan house and a Ruth in th' other, moy graciouz! and there's an Airthur in each, whatsomiver!"